SET MENU

3

Reborn as a Vending Machine, I Now Wander the DUNGEON

STORY BY
Hirukuma

ILLUSTRATION BY
Ituwa Kato

Hulemy

Reborn as a Vending Machine, I Now Wander the DUNGEON

3

Hirukuma

ILLUSTRATION BY
Ituwa Kato

YEN ON

NEW YORK

Reborn as a Vending Machine, I Now Wander the Dungeon

VOLUME 3

Hirukuma

Translation by Andrew Prowse
Cover art by Ituwa Kato

This book is a work of fiction. Names, characters, places, and incidents are the product of the author's imagination or are used fictitiously. Any resemblance to actual events, locales, or persons, living or dead, is coincidental.

JIDOU HANBAIKI NI UMAREKAWATTA ORE HA MEIKYUU WO SAMAYOU, Vol. 3
© 2017 Hirukuma, Ituwa Kato
First published in Japan in 2017 by KADOKAWA CORPORATION, Tokyo.
English translation rights arranged with KADOKAWA CORPORATION, Tokyo, through
TUTTLE-MORI AGENCY, INC., Tokyo.

English translation © 2018 by Yen Press, LLC

Yen On
1290 Avenue of the Americas
New York, NY 10104

Visit us at yenpress.com

facebook.com/yenpress yenpress.tumblr.com
twitter.com/yenpress instagram.com/yenpress

First Yen On Edition: December 2018

Yen On is an imprint of Yen Press, LLC.
The Yen On name and logo are trademarks of Yen Press, LLC.

The publisher is not responsible for websites (or their content) that are not owned by the publisher.

Library of Congress Cataloging-in-Publication Data
Names: Hirukuma, author. | Kato, Ituwa, illustrator. | Prowse, Andrew (Andrew R.), translator.
Title: Reborn as a vending machine, I now wander the dungeon / Hirukuma;
illustration by Ituwa Kato; translation by Andrew Prowse.
Other titles: Jidou hanbaiki ni umarekawatta ore wa meikyuu wo samayou. English
Description: First Yen On edition. | New York, NY: Yen On, April 2018–
Identifiers: LCCN 2018004692 | ISBN 9780316479110 (v. 1: pbk.) |
ISBN 9780316479134 (v. 2: pbk.) | ISBN 9780316479158 (v. 3: pbk.)
Classification: LCC PL871.I77 J5313 2018 | DDC 895.63/6—dc23
LC record available at https://lccn.loc.gov/2018004692

ISBNs: 978-0-316-47915-8 (paperback)
978-0-316-47916-5 (ebook)

1 3 5 7 9 10 8 6 4 2

LSC-C

Printed in the United States of America

Reborn as a Vending Machine, I Now Wander the DUNGEON

CONTENTS

Illustration: Ituwa Kato
Design Work: Yuuko Mukadeya + Kabuto Tanigome (Mushikago Graphics)

Characters

Boxxo

A former vending machine maniac.
He can sell any product he bought from a
vending machine in his past life.

Lammis

An energetic, sprightly, incredibly strong girl.
Has more power than she knows what to
do with. Boxxo's partner.

Hulemy

A talented magic-item engineer. Lammis's childhood friend; behaves like her older sister.

Shui

An informal archer. Depletes the Menagerie of
Fools's food budget with her huge appetite.

Director Bear

Director of the Hunters Association.
Deeply considerate of the people.

Shirley

Runs a business of the night.
A cordial person.

With our hunt for the Labyrinth stratum lord out of the way, the only thing left is to go back home—to the Clearflow Lake stratum.

I can't walk, so I'm having Lammis carry me, as always. If anyone else saw this short girl easily lugging a vending machine on her back, they'd probably think it was pretty bizarre. I don't feel strange about her hauling me around, and I have to wonder if that's a good thing. In the end, being on her back puts me at ease.

We're currently on our way to the settlement in the Labyrinth stratum where the transfer circle is located. But I have to say, we've got a big group here.

I look around at everyone again, thinking about how unique they all are.

First up is Lammis, with her blond hair featuring a side ponytail—not to mention the contrast between her adorable smile and ample chest. She's my most precious partner in this world.

Next is her childhood friend, Hulemy, with hair the color of milk tea and a fiery, masculine spirit. She seems to be sensitive about her much flatter chest, but I think there's actually some demand for that.

Then we have Director Bear, whose charisma affords him the impression of a dapper gentleman in a coat and hat, rather than a giant bear. He's easily the most reliable person—er, *bear*—in this alternate universe.

After him is Karios, a gatekeeper in the Clearflow Lake stratum, who has a girlfriend despite his stern face and shaved head. There's also his reticent partner, Gorth, sporting a square coif.

That just leaves the Menagerie of Fools and the Band of Gluttons.

I'll start with the Menagerie of Fools, one of the more well-known hunting teams in this world. Their captain, Kerioyl, looks exactly like a gunman in a Wild West film.

He's regularly accompanied by Vice Captain Filmina, a beautiful woman with wavy blue hair. She's always cool and collected, and she never hesitates to put him in his place when he goes off the rails.

Shui is the tomboyish girl with really short hair. Two of her most notable character traits are her bluntness and her incredible appetite.

The red-and-white twins, Red and White, look so similar that you wouldn't be able to tell them apart if not for their distinct hair colors. They're also easygoing.

Finally, we have the Voracious Devils, also known as the Band of Gluttons. This team consists of pouch-panda fiends, which are rare even in this world, but they're basically Tasmanian devil beast people.

Their leader, Mikenne, is the levelheaded one of the bunch.

Pell is the chubbiest and cutest of the four. His appetite is as impressive as Shui's.

Short has a slim build and black hair. Serving as their group's vice leader, he seems the most composed.

Suco, with her cute floppy ears, is the only female in the Band.

All the members of our group total fourteen people and one vending machine.

We'll apparently be staying a short time in the Labyrinth stratum settlement before returning to the Clearflow Lake stratum. We're going to help them trace an accurate copy of the map I recorded of this stratum, including the locations of traps.

People avoid the Labyrinth stratum due to its intricate passageways and terrible booby traps, so the Hunters Association is willing to put as much effort as they need into raising survival rates here as high as they can.

Until that's all settled, the Labyrinth stratum settlement will be my home away from home.

It seems like they already know the location and activation conditions for most of the traps on the biggest path through the labyrinth. Monsters appear occasionally, but we don't have any problems defeating them.

We arrive at the entrance of the labyrinth two days later without any notable incidents.

There's no gate at the entrance, nor any guards. As we leave the labyrinth, I start to see scattered buildings ahead, but it's a rather lonely sight.

Beyond the walls of the labyrinth stretches a vast wasteland, devoid of even a single blade of grass.

Structures dot the landscape—mostly simple log cabins and completely square stone houses. There aren't even any walls around the settlement... What do they do about monsters?

"It looks pretty dreary, doesn't it, Boxxo?" says Lammis.

"Welcome."

"Yeah. I wonder why it's so lifeless and lonely."

"You don't know, Lammis?" says Hulemy. "The Labyrinth stratum is really dangerous, but you can expect rewards that match the risks. Since the death rate here is abnormally high, there are a few hunters who managed to make so much money down here that they'll never be able to use it all."

I remember the Band of Gluttons talking about that, too.

"That's the sort of place this is," continues Hulemy. "Only two kinds of people come here—formidable hunters with genuine skill and dumbasses trying to get rich quick."

For no particular reason, her gaze wanders over to the Gluttons. The four are talking cheerfully among themselves as they march.

As to my determination on which category they fit into... Well, I'll keep that to myself.

"Hunters almost never come here, but the Hunters Association has to send enough workers to maintain this area's transfer circle," explains Hulemy. "It would be inconvenient if there weren't any inns or places to eat just because few people pass through. So they basically only have the Hunters Association building, an inn that doubles as a restaurant, a weapons and armor shop, and an item shop."

"Wow. Hulemy, you're so informed," says Lammis. "Wait, they call it a settlement, but it doesn't have any walls for defense. How come?"

"For whatever reason, the labyrinth's monsters never set foot outside the labyrinth. There aren't any monsters in the outer wasteland, either, so the settlement probably doesn't need walls."

"Still, the Association would like to see a few more hunters visit this stratum. Prior to this incident, generating interest has been a laborious task. Thanks to Boxxo's map, however, prospects are looking better. You have my thanks."

It was Director Bear who broke into the conversation. He must have been listening beside us, waiting for a good moment to chime in.

"There are far too many areas in this dungeon that we still don't fully understand. Our emergency response will be slow without a sufficient number of people stationed on each stratum. In the worst-case scenario, it could be too late by the time we're able to take action. We cannot allow things to reach such a state, especially with all stratum lords reviving of late. I cannot help having a bad premonition about all this."

This world is filled with things I don't understand. Encountering two stratum lords in such a short amount of time must not be possible under normal circumstances.

"Boxxo, we'll have you helping us create a map for the next few days, but we'll give you an additional reward for the scenery you preserved from the skies."

In that case, I have no complaints. Actually, I never had any to begin with. I was happy enough that he had brought Lammis along with the rest of the rescue party—even if I had already calculated that would happen.

Because of that, I'm not, to be honest, fully comfortable getting an additional reward, but I don't even have the language ability to politely turn him down, so I'll stay quiet and accept it.

Later, in the middle of our conversation, everyone suddenly stops walking. We must have reached our destination—the Hunters Association building in the Labyrinth stratum.

Unlike one in the Clearflow Lake stratum, this is an awfully small-scale building that looks more like a renovated two-story house. At best, it's quaint, and at worst…well, at least it's probably inexpensive.

Upon entering through the double doors, I see a counter by the wall and two round tables with several chairs. There's a bookshelf, too. That's about it for furniture.

Two women who probably work here sit on the opposite side of the counter, but besides them, the room is empty. As though they had nothing to do before we got here, one is reading a book, and the other is sleeping.

"Huh? Oh—Director Bommy! You've returned early. You found them already?"

One of the employees quickly let go of her book and rose in a fluster, bowing to Director Bear.

Her voice seemed to wake up the worker taking a nap, and after she gives a dazed look around, she bows in the same way as the woman next to her.

Director Bear's real name is Bommy, is it? It doesn't quite fit, if you ask me, so I'll keep referring to him as Director Bear in my thoughts.

"Kesha, Uliwa, I know you don't have much to do, but please remain a little more alert."

"I-I'm terribly sorry."

Kesha is the one with the black braid and glasses who was reading a book. The napping girl must be Uliwa. Her hair is cut short—she looks like the type of girl who would like athletic meets at school.

"Is the Labyrinth stratum director upstairs?" asks Director Bear.

"Yes, sir."

"All right. Captain, Vice Captain, Hulemy, and…Mikenne, could you all please come with me? Everyone else may rest here."

Lammis sets me down in a corner of the hall. It's been a while since I spent any time under a roof. Then again, as a vending machine, I'm fine being outdoors, too.

If it's break time for them, that means it's work time for me. I'm extremely familiar with everyone's preferences, so I line up all their favorites in my display. Having bought things from me many times before, they make their purchases one after another with practiced motions. Once they're done, they lay the snacks out on the round desks and start to unwind.

"E-excuse me, but what might that thing be?"

Before I realize it, the two employees from the reception area have approached; unable to hide their curiosity, they ask the Menagerie of Fools about me.

"Hmm? Oh, Boxxo? Um, he's an awesome magic item that you put coins into to buy whatever ya want."

I should have expected that my top customer in the Menagerie would praise me to the heavens. Thanks, Shui.

Seeing everyone else enjoying their food, the two reception employees audibly gulp.

"Let's buy something. We only ever eat at that cafeteria."

"You're right. The cafeteria food doesn't taste bad, but I'm sick of it…"

Well, they have only one eatery-slash-inn in this settlement. I'd get sick of it, too. Come to think of it, I wonder if the eatery-slash-inn is doing okay financially. Maybe they actually get subsidies from the Hunters Association or something along those lines.

After inspecting what the other people bought, the lady with the black braid and glasses purchases milk tea and a can of oden. The other one buys some corn soup and cup ramen.

They sniff at their purchases and poke the cans a bit, and after fiddling with this and that, they seem convinced that the items are harmless. Nervously, they each take a sip—and then their eyes pop open.

"Oh, this is better than I thought!"

"What is this? It sure goes down well. It's so sweet, I could get addicted."

Thank you for the glowing reviews. I've scored two new customers, so now I suppose I'll settle down and check on my points. I wonder if I have even more now that we've defeated a second stratum lord.

[Vending Machine: Boxxo—Rank 2]
DUR 200/200
TGH 50

STR 0
SPD 20
DEX 0
MAG 0
PT 517,654

{Features} Cold Retention, Heat Retention,
    Omnidirectional Vision, Hot-Water Dispenser (Cup
    Ramen Mode), Two-Liter Support, Candy-Roll
    Vending, Paint Change, Boxed-Item Support, Vending
    Machine Surveillance Camera, Solar Power
    Generation, Wheels, Electronic Billboard, LCD
    Panel, Oxygen Vending Machine, Magazine Vending
    Machine, Ice Vending Machine, Dry Ice Vending
    Machine, Gas Vending Machine, Balloon Vending
    Machine, Vegetable Vending Machine, Egg Vending
    Machine, Cardboard Vending Machine, Coin-Operated
    Vacuum Cleaner, High-Pressure Washer
{Blessings} Force Field
{Inventory} Octo Croc Coin

I, uh, have so many features that I'm not really sure what's going on anymore. Most have been helpful and have worked the way I wanted, but the electronic bulletin board was a mistake. I didn't think about how I could have put whatever letters I wanted onto it—and if I had, I probably would have been able to speak freely to begin with.

There might be a different way to use it in the future, so I'll keep it in the back of my mind.

Other than that, I increased my durability and toughness quite a bit, but I can't get a proper sense for how tough or durable I am right now.

I'm aware that Lammis's running tackle damaged me because of her Might. I'd like to take a hit from a really strong enemy at some point, just to see, but even if I never get the chance, it's not like I'll have any complaints.

Anyway, back to my points. They're above 510,000. I got close to a million from defeating the Octo Croc, but this time, I received about half that. I have trouble deciding whether that means the Flame Skeletitan was just worth less points than the Octo Croc or if it's because the others racked up damage on it before I landed the finishing blow.

Either way, I know one thing—I don't have a million points. If I do reach a million again, I should definitely take a Blessing this time. Yeah.

With that fallacious vow in my heart, I finally relax in this place shielded from wind and rain, and for the first time since falling into the Labyrinth stratum, I decide to sleep.

Not Quite the Ideal Hero

Since coming to the Labyrinth stratum, I've gained a host of new regulars. The married couple who runs the weapons and armor shop, a parent and child pair from the inn, the Hunters Association receptionists—most of the residents have started buying things from me on a daily basis.

Still, there are way too few people living on this stratum. It may be deserted, but with only ten or so people, how do they stay in business? At least, that's what an outsider like me was needlessly worried about, but Lammis had the same question—she asked the receptionists, and they solved the mystery.

My prediction was actually correct—it seems the Hunters Association is paying them a fixed monthly income. That means even if they get no customers, they've been guaranteed a living wage, at the very least.

That changes things. There are probably a lot of people who would endure this environment if they could get money even without working.

They welcome the boredom to a certain extent, but it can drag on for a long time. The more of a hardworking person you are, the more restlessness and anxiety you seem to feel when there's nothing to do.

That's why whenever hunters pass through, they're always treated very hospitably.

We won't be leaving the Labyrinth stratum anytime soon, so the residents' faces are filled with life and excitement as they cater to us—almost too much—every day.

◆

Three days after arriving in the stratum, the Menagerie of Fools headed to another stratum to scope it out, telling us they'll invite us there once they've finished gathering information.

Director Bear, too, would apparently cause several problems if he didn't return to the Clearflow Lake stratum soon, so he's already returned there. I'm sure he has a lot of paperwork piled up.

The ones who stayed behind are Lammis and Hulemy, as well as the Band of Gluttons, staying nearby at Director Bear's request. As we each prepared to start working in earnest tomorrow, by an unusual twist of fate, another hunter arrived at the stratum.

He was a lone hunter—a handsome young man with blond hair, blue eyes, and an androgynous appearance. He wore a full suit of jet-black armor that was awfully shiny, as though the color were painted on, as he walked through the Hunters Association's doors.

He has it all: a handsome face, slender arms and legs, and a suit of jet-black armor with a large sword on his back.

He's like the complete package of every woman's ideals, the kind of character who would appear in a certain game famous for its super-beautiful CG work. I can't blame the receptionists for staring at him.

I never thought such beauty could actually exist. Alternate worlds are truly ludicrous.

"Excuse me. I just arrived on this stratum today. Would you happen to have a detailed map of the labyrinth?"

His manner is gentle, and his voice sounds clear. I haven't spotted any flaws yet. It may be strange for a vending machine to feel jealous about this, but if I were a person, standing next to him would cause me pain as a member of the same sex.

"Y-yes. If you'll wait three more days, we plan to have a brand-new accurate map completed."

So that's the face of a woman smitten. I'm the type who doesn't believe in love at first sight, but given how attractive he is, I can't really blame her. Come to think of it...

Curious about Lammis and Hulemy, who were having a drink near me, I look over...and they're kicking up a row, staring at the young man.

"Hulemy, look! That man is so pretty it's like he came out of a painting."

"Whoa, you're right. He's a knockout."

I was a little worried that even their hearts had been swayed when faced with that level of handsomeness—but their reactions are pretty average. It doesn't seem like they've fallen for him, but rather, they are simply impressed, kind of like they've stumbled upon a celebrity on the street. Still, I think a perfect ten like him would have no trouble captivating any woman.

"Three days? All right. I'll come back in three days, then."

Flashing one last smile, as pure and crisp as a spring wind, he disappears through the doors.

Even after he's out of sight, the two receptionists keep waving. That must be the pretty-boy magic at work.

Women are so simple and easily fooled by looks—is something I'm not cynical enough to say. Men are easily won over by beautiful women with large breasts, so I think it goes both ways.

Even from another man's perspective, I can't blame them, given just how good-looking that guy was. My jealousy starts to feel more and more ridiculous. Besides, I'm a vending machine, so human appearances don't matter to me.

"He was like the heroes in old stories."

"Lammis, you've built up a glorified idea of heroes. They're never crazy good-looking. The famous hunters are all mostly brawny older guys—real muscle heads."

Lammis stands shocked, her ideals shattered. Ignorance is bliss, I say.

"B-but what about that famous hunter with a hundred Blessings and the favor of God?! I heard stories that she's a downright pretty gal, and I really look up to her!"

Once again, Lammis's excitement causes her accent to leak out.

A hundred Blessings? That's amazing. How many points would

that cost? Wait… Come to think of it, I can spend points to acquire features and Blessings, but do other people, like hunters, work on a point system, too? I'm surprised I didn't think of the question earlier.

I've gotten to thinking this sort of system is completely natural, but do hunters get stronger this way when they defeat monsters? Unfortunately, this isn't something I can ask them with the set phrases available to me.

"Oh, the chick with the favor of God? There are still books and eyewitnesses who say she was really a beautiful and kind person. But she never stayed in one place for long, so nobody knows anything about her beyond the stories and legends that've spread all over the place."

Wow, she must be really cool. An unidentified wandering beauty—and a powerful character, at that. If someone used her as material for a story, it would definitely be popular.

"That's a relief. I'm aimin' to be just like her, after all!"

"Well, that pretty boy might be one of those special people, too. If he's challenging the Labyrinth stratum by himself, he's gotta be pretty strong."

He wouldn't need to be that skilled with his appearance—he'd have female hunters lining up for miles hoping to join his team. But he's going it alone anyway. Maybe that speaks to the depth of his talent.

He could have had other team members waiting outside, but for some reason, he doesn't strike me as the type to let other people into his inner circle. His mannerisms are gentle and polite—but also like he's intentionally keeping some distance between others and himself. Could just be my imagination, though.

Still, it doesn't matter to me what he's like on the inside as long as he doesn't mess with my friends.

Night falls, and with no entertainment facilities on the Labyrinth stratum, everyone usually turns in early.

The inn has no shortage of free rooms. It's where Lammis and the others are staying. From the outside, I see the light in their window go out. They must be going to sleep early.

I'm standing in front of the inn, lazily gazing at the settlement. I probably could have asked someone to bring me inside, but I'm worried my weight would break the floor, so I decided to stay outside.

I'm completely used to my vending machine body now, so I don't mind watching things outdoors like this, either. In fact, my body seems oddly accustomed to it.

I feel like both my body and mind are entirely vending machine now... I guess that's not a bad thing.

I turn on my night-electricity-conservation mode and lower my light to a dim glow. There are no sources of light nearby, meaning I still stand out a lot.

Still, this Labyrinth stratum is too barren for me. It may be safe outside the walls, but it's all wasteland, unsuitable for raising crops. There are no monsters, but there are also no animals. It seems like a worthless bit of land, but I'm pretty sure there's actually value in using it.

If this were modern Japan or some such place, people could probably make an industrial district here. Of course, maybe it would be too difficult for normal people to seek work in the dungeon, where you never know what'll happen.

There's still a lot I don't understand about the labyrinth in the first place. The dungeons I know of don't have skies, and a single dungeon floor usually isn't this vast. The scale is completely different.

And the stuff about getting any wish granted if you clear the lowest stratum seems like a hoax. Of course, taking into account the kind of being who would create such an absurd fantasy world, I can't say it's impossible.

Hmm. As a vending machine, I'd like to focus solely on my sales, but that wish doesn't seem very realistic anymore.

As I continued along my fairly serious train of thought, my surroundings suddenly brightened. Given the hour, it should have been dark and deserted all around. Did someone come out of the inn?

The double doors fly open, and an attractive person walks out—the noteworthy young man from this afternoon.

With a wobbling, unreliable gait, he slips in front of me. His expression, illuminated by my light, is lifeless, without even a hint of the relaxed, confident attitude he showed earlier today. His eyes are wandering, and his body is trembling.

"Ahhhh, man, I'm freaking out. Why does everyone always have to stare at me like that? Ughhh, that was scary. I heard there weren't a lot of people on this stratum, but there are so maaany…"

Um…? Did this young man just start shooting off complaints about something pitiful? Hold on, does this mean his attitude from earlier was a facade, and this is his true self?

"Agh, I can't do this anymore… I hate talking to people… Give me a break. Urghhhh…"

The sigh he gave sounded like his spirit leaving his body through his mouth. Does he have social anxiety? Is he playing the perfect good-looking character in order to hide that? He might be traveling alone because of it. But… Suddenly, I start to empathize with him.

"No, no, no. Mom always said to approach things with positivity—and not to always assume things are going bad. I have to be positive—positive!"

I watch as he takes a few deep breaths and then clenches his fists. I kind of want to cheer him on.

I remember that cacao beans have something in them that calms the automatic nervous system and helps people relax. In that case, I'll stock some hot cocoa as a new product.

"Welcome."

"Waaaah! That was terrifying! Wait, what—what—what is this?!"

I seem to have surprised him quite a bit—he jumped a good ten feet straight up. His physical abilities are incredible. The reaction gives me an urge to tease him, but that would be mistaking the insignificant for the essential.

"Insert coins."

"Ah, um… Is this the box that was at the Hunters Association building today? If I remember correctly, it's a mysterious object that lets you shop. The pouch-panda fiends were buying things from it."

With his upper body bent backward to a somewhat concerning degree, he dexterously approaches. His fear is plain on his face. I'm the cause, of course, but I do hope the hot cocoa calms him down.

I line the cans of hot cocoa all along my bottom row so they stand out.

"Um, this is where you put the coins in, right? And then, I think I just have to press the bump underneath the item I want."

After confirming the coin sliding inside me, I make the buttons light up to show that he can purchase something now. Come on—choose the hot cocoa!

"I wonder what I should pick. These cups have a picture of brown liquid pouring on them, so they must be drinks. If there's a lot of them, they have to be popular. If it's anything like the tea I used to drink at home...I'll go with that."

I'm happy my scheme worked, guiding him to pick the hot cocoa, but he sure does talk to himself a lot. Come to think of it, one of my friends said that when people work from home and don't see anyone much during their day-to-day, they start talking to themselves more.

He seems to have social anxiety, so maybe he doesn't actually get as many chances to interact with people as I first assumed.

"Wow, it's so warm. Um, let's see. To open it, I pull this up... It worked!"

His innocently happy face makes him look adorable. When he presents himself well, he's hot, but if his smile is cute like this, it would be the older, big sister–type ladies falling for him.

"Mmm! It's so sweet and delicious! And it really calms me down for some reason. What a wonderful magic item this is. It doesn't require me to talk to anyone, so buying things is easy!"

Please don't stare at me so ravenously. It doesn't feel bad to be wanted and valued so highly, but my home is at Lammis's side.

"Those girls were the owners, weren't they? I'll negotiate with them tomorrow," he says, cradling the can of hot cocoa carefully in both hands and disappearing back into the inn.

I don't think his negotiations will get him anywhere, but it's splendid that he didn't try to steal me by force. Personally, I like people like him, but I probably won't have any more opportunities to meet him after this.

After all, we'll be moving out on a different request tomorrow.

"Boxxo, Mishuel is going to be coming with us for the request!"

"I'm looking forward to working with you, Boxxo."

The next morning, Lammis bursts out in front of me, and that's the first thing that comes out of her mouth.

Such a sudden development... I think he's a likeable young man, but for some reason, I feel a little apprehensive about it.

The hottie standing next to Lammis gives me a smile and puts out his hand before realizing I can't shake it and instead scratches his head in embarrassment.

The Periphery

In the back of the buar cart provided by Director Bear rides Hulemy and the Band of Gluttons, while Lammis, with me on her back, and the young man are walking alongside it.

"Ha-ha. I see."

"But you really were planning on exploring the inside, huh?" says Lammis.

"Oh, y'know..."

"And why not? We've got a powerful hunter with us, so we'll be able to deal with all sorts of terrible situations. We'll be counting on ya," says Hulemy.

"Ha-ha. I see."

"I never thought I'd be able to travel with the Reclusive Black Flash. It's an honor!"

"Ha-ha. Is that so?"

For anyone who didn't know about the incident last night, he would seem like an agreeable young man, responding with a relaxed, cool smile...but on closer examination, it's clear his cheeks are slightly tense, and he's mostly repeating the same thing for every response. You should learn a few more variations, Mishuel.

At Director Bear's request, we're advancing along the giant laby-rinth's periphery. To our left is its towering outer wall. To our right, a vast, barren wasteland. The enemies never come out of the labyrinth, and no creatures live outside it.

The danger is pretty low for this request, which is why the director figured we'd be fine with just Lammis, Hulemy, and the Band of Gluttons.

Still, with all the strange things happening lately, anything can occur. Though it was an odd request, the director had approved Mishuel joining us as someone known far and wide to be powerful—which brings us to the present.

"Hulemy, he said it would take about a month to do a full circuit around the periphery, right?" asks Lammis.

"That's how long it took the hunters assigned to investigating it a year ago, but taking measurements based on Boxxo's image will make it less than three weeks, I think. I bet they took their time on purpose to charge more reward money."

Ahh, I see. If a job is safe and you get a reward based on how many days it took, it's not strange that some hunters would think that way.

"This mission is perfect for us, since we have Boxxo, who can supply us with unlimited food. The director originally wanted to ask the Band of Gluttons for this, since they have an established reputation for quickness and vitality, but then there would have been a food problem."

Fast-moving and easily adaptable to any environment in the wild... The investigation seems suited for the Band of Gluttons, but their greatest obstacle is ensuring they have enough food.

That's why Lammis and I ended up going with them, with Hulemy in charge of the more detailed investigations and analyses, like whether the walls have deteriorated any further, whether the nearby environment has changed at all, and if she can see any signs that something strange might happen in the future.

The job is simple—we follow the outer wall at a relaxed pace, almost like we're on a leisurely trip. But we've been caught up in so many unexpected happenings that it's hard not to be cautious.

"Well then—I'll bring up the rear, just to be safe."

The sudden voice snaps me back to the present.

With natural motions, Mishuel leaves and moves to the tail end of our party. But after making sure nobody has their eyes on him, he breathes a sigh of relief.

Well, my eyes are on him, but what he doesn't know won't hurt him. Still, if he's habitually this nervous around other people, why did he come with us on this mission?

I thought he'd approached Lammis with the offer to buy me, a vending machine...but that deal went south somewhere along the way, and here we are. I still have my reservations about him, though they don't enter the realm of distrust, so I'll keep an attentive watch over him.

After moving to the rear, Mishuel walks in silence, slightly downcast unless someone turns around to take a peek at him. I realized only after watching his face closely that his mouth is moving oddly.

Is he talking to himself again? I focus, trying to make out what he's saying.

"During this...one month...as much as I can...women...and pouch-pandas...who I'm not used to...be able to...act naturally..."

I catch only pieces, but I have a good idea of what he's saying. He must want to improve his social anxiety a little by traveling with us—a group consisting of only women and Tasmanian devil people.

The members of the Band of Gluttons are quite different from humans, so I can understand them being easier to talk to. But wouldn't women make him more nervous than men? Then again, there are a lot of stern-faced male hunters out there... Karios and Gorth, for example, would probably make weak-kneed children cry on sight.

Hmm. I'll have to help him out, then. When he buys something, I'll make sure to speak to him. I hope that gets him a little more used to a male voice.

Anyway, let's set him aside for now. I look around but see nothing.

Just the wall and the wasteland. The scenery is exactly the same, and there's no sign that we've gotten anywhere. Is this going to continue for almost a month? Alone, I'd get fed up with it, but with the soul-soothing Band of Gluttons along with Lammis and Hulemy, it shouldn't be a struggle.

When lunchtime swings around, everyone buys food from me, then they go off to eat wherever they please. Into groups, actually—three to be precise.

The childhood friends, Lammis and Hulemy. The Band of Gluttons. And Mishuel, on his own.

At this rate, Mishuel will continue being the odd man out. He looks lonely. Lammis and Hulemy had casually invited him to eat with them, but he gently refused, his face a smiling mask, a perfect guard for the extreme shyness inside.

It looks like sitting down for a meal with others is a high hurdle for him. I hope he can eat lunch with us normally before this month is over.

—But still, I feel a twinge of apprehension when I think about such an attractive man hanging out with Lammis or Hulemy.

People can say whatever they want, but they're weak to good looks. The two act like they have no interest in him, but it's only normal to feel attracted to such a good-looking guy right next to them. A beautiful woman and a handsome man paint a pretty picture. It wouldn't be strange for one—no, for *both* of them to fall for him.

Wait, what use is it for a vending machine to feel jealous? The matters of the heart are no business of mine. It's weird that I even have this on my mind.

Besides, I'm pretty sure Mishuel isn't a threat anyway. Having watched how he acts and talks triggers my protective instincts and makes me want to cheer him on.

"T-tomorrow, I'll eat my food three feet closer to everyone else. Yeah. I have to try harder."

His pitiable words are carried to me on the winds of the wastes— Yeah, wanting to root for this guy is only human.

On the surface, he looks like he's happily eating his food, but he's smiling only when he senses someone watching him. He needs to smile more naturally—his cheeks are starting to twitch a little.

At this point, I feel like it would be easier if he just came out and said he was bad at interacting with people, but he probably can't, which is why he wears his false mask. I wonder what kind of family environment you'd have to be raised in to turn out like that.

After lunch is over, we set off on our leisurely procession around the periphery.

It's so peaceful. I'm very much aware that I can't let my guard down, so I won't relax more than I need to, but it would be nice if nothing happened.

Ever since coming to this world, extreme, life-threatening events have occurred again and again. Laid-back days like this are what life should really be like for a vending machine.

And just as I had hoped, the first day is about to end with us having done nothing but walk.

The nights in this stratum aren't cold, and the temperature doesn't change throughout the year, so the Band of Gluttons snore the night away on the ground, their full bellies exposed. Their sleeping faces are adorable, too. I'll just record them on my surveillance camera for later enjoyment.

Lammis and Hulemy appear to be sleeping in the covered cart bed. I can just make out their faint breaths. Mishuel and I are keeping watch for the others, but the signs of mental exhaustion from his constant worrying about everyone else looking at him all day are showing—he's sitting cross-legged on the ground, and he's close to losing consciousness. Several times, his head droops, then he opens his eyes and looks around.

"Ah! No, no. Everyone told me it would be fine and Boxxo would keep watch, but... Ughhhh, maaan, that was nerve-racking. They're both so pretty, and the Band of Gluttons are so cute. It took everything I had to keep my cool. Oh, come to think of it... I wonder if this boxy magic item really does have a mind."

Dubiously, he looks at me.

Well, it's probably normal not to be able to believe it without seeing it. The two girls are too sharp-witted, and the Band of Gluttons were lured in by all the food.

He puts a hand to his chin and brings his face so close his forehead almost touches me. He's staring as though trying to peer inside me. Even a vending machine would be embarrassed.

"Welcome."

"Ah, yes, hello. G-good evening."

Personally, I think his mild-mannered, timid state leaves a better impression than his usual "hot-guy mode." At heart, he's just a shy young man.

"Um, what should I buy? Oh, yes—that sweet, relaxing drink was really good. I'm always nervous even when I'm buying things, but with this magic-item box, I don't have to worry about other people watching."

Yup, that's right. I get where you're coming from—a store clerk can really make you nervous. The carefree ability to buy things is one of a vending machine's merits.

As Mishuel grips his cocoa and exhales in relief, I watch his face in profile for no particular reason. At times like these, he looks younger than his age.

The mood he gives off and the carefree expression he makes when his guard is down would make him a smash hit with cougars. I can say for certain that if someone had *shota* inclinations, one look and they'd be done for. Normally one would be jealous of *something* about him given his level of beauty, but when I look at him, I want to help him out. Maybe it's a personal magnetism.

And so, another week passed without incident—not a fight to be had. It seems like Mishuel has closed the distance just a little bit between himself and the rest of our party.

It's probably the result of the Band of Gluttons being adorable and Lammis being so sociable. However, he still treats them with the politeness you would use with a stranger—he's never talked to them in his truly unreserved state.

To be honest, a small part of me balks at the idea of Mishuel fixing his social anxiety and getting too close with Lammis and Hulemy.

I don't like feeling this way. Ugh. A vending machine being jealous is just weird.

I've been paying the most attention to Mishuel, but Lammis is acting rather strange today. Her eyes are empty, and her gait is heavy. It looks like it's taking everything just to walk.

"Hey, what's the matter, Lammis?" asks Hulemy. "If you don't feel well, you can ride in the cart and bring Boxxo with you."

"Welcome." That's right. We don't have to hurry for this request, so there's no need to push yourself.

Hulemy is leaning out of the cart, beckoning to her. Considering her issues with physical exertion, the spot in the cart naturally went to Hulemy, but Lammis hasn't taken a breather even once.

"Hmm? I'm okay. Fit as can be."

You can wave it off all you want, but you don't look okay. Your normally lively smile has a huge shadow cast over it.

Still, I wonder what the problem could be. If she had a cold, I'd think she would have been sneezing or coughing, but she's not even congested. Every once in a while, she'll rub her lower stomach, so maybe it's some abdominal pain. My items couldn't have caused it, right? Then what is it?

"L-Lammis, you shouldn't force yourself. You should rest for now."

"Huh—? *Hya!*"

Mishuel was trying to lift Lammis up on his back, so I changed into a cardboard vending machine. That way, even he can carry us, and he brings us to the cart with light steps.

Hmm. Lammis normally does the carrying, and now she's the one being carried. Ahh, that murky feeling is starting to come up again. I should be grateful for Mishuel acting out of such kind consideration. I'm the worst.

"Boxxo, you're lighter than I thought."

No, no, that's because I'm cardboard right now. If I was my regular vending machine self, you'd be buried underground at the moment.

Lammis is trying to resist, but she doesn't seem to have much energy, and Mishuel places her on the cart easily. She can't even muster the willpower to object, so she gives up and sits down.

If I had arms and legs, would that have been my job? Going back to being human… I might want to seriously think about it.

"Hulemy, can I ask you to take care of her?"

"Sure thing. Leave it to me."

With Lammis left in her caring hands, I shouldn't have anything to worry about.

Hulemy removes me from her back and gently puts me outside the cart. I go back to my original vending machine form and, for the time being, stock some sports drinks.

I drop one into my compartment, and Mishuel immediately reacts.

"I think this is a gift from Boxxo," he says, putting it on the corner of the cart.

He's thoughtful, and he's good-looking. Yup, there isn't a single area I can beat him in.

"Sheesh. You always push yourself right up to the limit. Here, take off your clothes. I'll change them for you."

"Y-you don't have to do that. I can do it myself—"

"Quit trying to pretend everything's fine. You're obviously worn-out. The kindness of others is something you should accept without complaining."

I can hear the moans and groans of resistance, but it sounds like Hulemy has the advantage this time. Lammis must be really weak right now. We'll have her rest quietly for a while—

"Ohhh! Wait, there's blood! You idiot! Why did you keep qui... qui...? Oh."

Wait, she's losing blood?! Did she get hurt somewhere?! Dammit, how could I not have noticed? She was carrying me the whole time!

"Ah, ah, ah, ah..."

As Hulemy continues to stutter in surprise, I hear Lammis simply repeating the syllable *Ah* like she doesn't know what to do. She's not acting like she's in pain—her face is bright red.

"Lammis, is it your period?!"

"Ughhh, you dummyyy!"

How could you yell that, Hulemy? Now Lammis is crying out in despair, the poor thing.

Mishuel looks away, one hand to his mouth in surprise, but for my part, it now makes perfect sense how she'd suddenly grown so weak.

She's had days like this about once a month in the past. I'm sorry for not realizing it sooner.

"What's a 'period'? Is it a food?"

"I don't know. I've never heard of it, either."

"I think it has something to do with women. Suco, do you know what it is?"

"Um, well. It happens a lot with female humans and some types of monkeys. Apparently, it's a condition specific to females where blood comes out of their lower abdomen.'

The Band of Gluttons are huddled up, whispering like older boys in elementary school.

Come to think of it, I heard once that creatures apart from humans and certain animals don't experience menstruation, and even the ones that do have only very minor issues. They must not be very familiar with the topic.

"Sheesh, Lammis, don't be so reckless. Your periods get bad, don't they? Ahh, your underwear and cloth are covered in blood. If you don't change this cloth out with a clean one, it could make you really sick."

"Okay…"

"It's nothing to be ashamed about. Having children is something only women can do. Treat yourself better."

I can't see what it is they're doing, but based on their voices, it sounds like Hulemy has gotten the whole thing under control. Just listening to their conversation makes me restless, like I'm doing something bad.

Men aren't good with this sort of thing. I can't exactly speak on the issue. In terms of what I can do to help... I can give them clean towels, and then— Oh, you know what? There is something I can do.

From my features list, I choose Manually Operated Sanitation Vending Machine and change my form.

My body becomes sheer white, as though to evoke an image of cleanliness, and it slims down quite a bit, too. As the term *manually operated* would imply, this vending machine doesn't need electricity. Instead, you put in the coins, then crank a lever to get the products out.

There are two main products this vending machine sells: sanitary napkins and masks. I think there are versions that sell tissue packets, too.

If you're a woman, you've probably seen them near the bathrooms in department stores, stations, schools, and the like. I don't think many men have had the chance to see one.

Then, you may ask, why can I, a vending machine who is restricted to only stocking products I've bought before, provide these? ...W-well, it's nothing to feel guilty about.

One of my relatives was in the cleaning business, and I just have some experience working part-time for them during my school days. I recall a distant memory—having to clean the women's bathroom and seeing this vending machine for the first time, then buying its contents out of pure interest without even knowing what was inside. Anyway, that's not important right now.

"Oh. Boxxo, what's up? You got thinner—and whiter. If you transformed now, it must mean something. I'll put in a coin."

Whenever it comes to Lammis and Hulemy, it's easy to get my point across. Seriously, thank you.

Hulemy pulls the lever, removes the product, and then looks at it closely for a bit. She tilts her head, not seeming to really get it.

"Huh, this is strange. I don't think I need this clear bag. This cloth feels strange to the touch... Wait, is it paper?"

She pokes and prods it as she studies it, then appears to understand from the situation what I want her to do. Finally, after seeming to fail a few times, she manages to use it properly.

"This thing's amazing. The absorption is incredible. With this, we won't have to worry even on days when it's super-heavy."

Hulemy soaks up water from a bottle with her newly purchased sanitary napkins in admiration.

Menstruation is such a true-to-life problem. Fantasy stories often feature a lot of female adventurers, but it seems like they have struggles of their own to deal with behind the scenes.

I would never have understood it if I hadn't been reborn in another world.

"I guess I'll get some water from Boxxo to wash your bloodstained pants and underwear."

"Oh, I can wash them for you."

"No, I don't think that would be a good idea. At the end of the day, Lammis is technically a girl. I'll do it."

"You didn't need to add 'technically'..."

From my vantage point next to the cart, I see Mishuel, completely unfazed, attempt to ask Hulemy to give him the dirty underwear and pants. I can't decide if I should be impressed about that or critical. You'd think a man would be a little resistant to the idea.

I've heard bloodstains are tough to get out, so I add a new feature.

This is something I've been considering for a while. I change into a coin-operated, fully automatic washer dryer. It's the kind of washing machine with a door, like in laundromats.

I've been concerned about the unhygienic lives of hunters, who only pack maybe one change of clothes, since any more would be too much of a hindrance. I figured they'd be happy if they had a chance to wash their clothes during monster-slaying quests and other missions.

For now, I pop open my round door, trying to motion to throw the laundry inside. Nobody enjoys the idea of hand-washing underwear with blood on them, after all.

Actually, now that I'm thinking about it calmly, isn't this situation a little risky? They'll be putting women's clothing in me to be washed... Uh, well, I'm a machine, so I don't feel guilty about it, and I'm not a pervert, so everything's fine. Definitely fine.

"This is a strange-looking form," says Lammis. "I wonder what it is."

"Is Boxxo telling us to put the dirty clothes inside?"

"Welcome."

"Right, then, I'm actually gonna put 'em in, okay?"

"Huh? You're going to put my underwear in Boxxo?"

I hear Lammis's confused voice, but— Look, I'm a machine, so you don't have to worry.

This will be a test run, so I'll give it to you for free. There's an automatic detergent injector, so after they throw in the clothes, all we have to do is wait. It's possible to adjust the settings to determine how to wash them and the length of time, too, but I'll take care of all those controls.

Mishuel, who looks like he's enjoying watching the clothes being washed, sidles right up to the glass to peer inside. The Band of Gluttons, watching him, grow curious, and eventually they all end up watching the washing machine spin round and round as well. What is going on here?

With this washing machine's specs, it should take thirty to forty minutes to finish. However, I've increased my speed, so it finishes in about ten. Increasing my speed was the right move. I can only change forms for two hours, which means I wouldn't be able to use this more than once unless I shortened the time.

When the sound plays to signal that it's finished, the Band of Gluttons jump back and cry out with a *"Vaaaaaa!"* of surprise. Their roaring is another thing I've gotten used to.

After I open the door, Hulemy hesitantly sticks a hand inside, pulls out the freshly washed pants and underwear, and holds them aloft. They flap in the wind blowing across the wasteland.

Hulemy, you shouldn't hold up underwear so casually like that. Everyone can see. Lammis is embarrassed—I can hear her making noise from the cart.

"This is amazing! They're perfectly white!"

Mishuel yells out excitedly when he sees the washed clothes. He grabs my washing machine body, then shakes it violently. Uh, he's more enthralled by all this than I expected him to be.

"Let's wash our other dirty clothes, too! I'll put everything in but my armor. Everyone else, please give me whatever you need washed!"

Without any time for me to stop him, Mishuel takes dirty laundry out of his backpack and starts throwing it inside the washing machine. Even Hulemy undresses inside the cart, then pokes her face out—she's in a single piece of underwear at the moment—and throws the rest of her clothes into the washer.

She has only a blanket covering her, but still, she doesn't seem conscious of the fact that Mishuel is a member of the opposite sex.

The Band of Gluttons have their jackets peeled off by Mishuel and are left standing there in just their shoes in dazed confusion. They can't keep up with the situation.

"The process of cleaning the dirt off is just great, isn't it? Tidying your room works the same way, but isn't seeing clothes get clean the best feeling? The maid at my house almost never lets me do it, so I'm having a lot of fun now."

Ah, so that's why he was watching the inside of the washing machine with his eyes sparkling like that. I'm happy he's happy. His remark reveals the fact that he has at least one maid in his house, which means he's high enough on the social ladder to employ them, right?

Still, even though only the tightly wound Mishuel is present, how are the young girls faring with their healthy bodies stripped down to their underwear and exposed? Lammis is half-naked right now, isn't she? It looks like she feels too crappy to notice it, though.

Mishuel has taken up a position where he can't see inside the cart, but I can see them quite well.

This is a good opportunity, so why don't I observe them in their underwear? If it clues me in to their fashion sense, I might be able to use that to expand my selection of products in the future. Underwear is a product, too, and I'll probably end up selling it to Shirley at some point. That's my only goal here—no ulterior motive in particular. No ulterior motives whatsoever. Not a scrap.

Well, I said "observe," but unlike modern Japan, the underwear here doesn't come in elaborate designs, either.

On top, what she's wearing isn't a brassiere but rather a blue cloth wrap.

For such a small frame, Lammis's two fiendishly giant breasts are no match for gravity, and they're being crushed against her chest. They're always being compressed by her leather armor, so they've never given such an intense impression until now. But with her not wearing much anymore, they pack one heck of a punch. She's lying on her back, but you can still tell at a glance that they're extraordinarily large.

"Lammis, did your breasts get bigger again?"

"Did…did they? I don't really know."

After staring hard at the weakened Lammis's chest, Hulemy's gaze moves to her own before she gives a short, defeated sigh.

She only has a black cloth wrapped around her chest, and it's close to perfectly flat. Her shapely lower half is sufficiently thick, but it looks like her chest is more concerning for her as a woman.

Personally, big or small—it's not a problem for me. But male instincts do tend to dictate that your eyes are drawn to the big-breasted women first. I guess it's natural women would care about it.

In this situation, a man should be excited and happy—but I'm a vending machine, so what do you want me to do? Or rather, a washing machine at the moment. There would be problems if I had too much libido in this form, so complaining about it would be a strange proposition.

After the washing and drying is done, everyone puts on their freshly cleaned clothes, satisfied at the faint scent of detergent as well as how they're warm to the touch.

"Why don't we take the day to rest?" suggests Mishuel.

"Good plan," agrees Hulemy. "It's only a little past noon, but a day off once in a while is fine, right?"

It looks like they decided not to move for the rest of the day out of consideration for Lammis's health. The Band of Gluttons proceed to lie on the ground and bask in the sun.

Mishuel's appetite for washing hasn't seemed to disappear yet, and he wonders if he could remove the covering from the cart and wash that. Hulemy seems to be reading a book, peering over at the sleeping Lammis every once in a while to make sure she's fine.

Okay then, what should I do? For now, I'll go back to my usual

vending machine form. Oh, and now Mishuel is making a clearly disappointed face.

Right—now that I have a surplus of points, I could also test out what kind of effects status changes will have.

My vending machine stats are durability, toughness, strength, speed, dexterity, and magic.

I don't need to verify at this point what durability and toughness do. Speed makes all my functions go faster, so I could increase that more in the future.

The problem is what's left over: strength, dexterity, and magic. Magic, at least, won't increase even if I spend points, so I rule that out.

Which brings me to strength. What would "strength" be for a vending machine? At the moment, I don't have any vending machine forms that require physical power. If I learn how to sprout arms and legs and move under my own power, then the stat might be essential, but I don't think there's any use for it right now.

That leaves dexterity…which I don't really understand. Will it make me able to do more precise things? Right now, I can't find any features that would require precision, so I don't feel any need to increase that, either.

Both need ten thousand points to increase by ten, so it would be a waste to dump them into stats I don't know how to use.

In the end, all I do is think about it. The rest of the day goes by without me increasing any of my stats.

Mishuel

"I'm sorry for causing you trouble, everyone."

When morning comes, Lammis looks quite a bit better. The first thing out of her mouth is an apology, and she bows her head deeply.

Everyone was preparing for breakfast, but Lammis climbs down from the cart and prances over to us.

"Oh, you're feeling better? Still, don't get too ahead of yourself."

"Y-yes, please don't force yourself. Look, Boxxo gave us some fresh sponech."

Incidentally, *sponech* is spinach. A lot of the vegetables here aren't any different from the ones in Japan; the names are the only things that diverge. I give them canned raisin bread, too. I've heard raisins are one of the best sources for iron.

"Everyone, I'm sorry for not telling you I wasn't feeling well."

"So that was why I smelled blood. I thought you were hiding raw meat on you," states Mikenne, tilting his head. His companions nod in the same way. I knew Tasmanian devils had a sharp sense of smell, but I never thought they'd be able to sniff out someone's period.

"Women are already at a disadvantage when it comes to the hunting business. This ain't a job we need to rush, so take it easy."

"Th-that's right. We're all here for one another."

"Thanks. I'll remember that."

Huh? It's still somewhat suspicious, but Mishuel's taking part in a conversation without adopting his usual cool-guy mode. Has hastily taking care of things and washing the clothes without giving his social anxiety a chance to activate lowered the barriers around his heart a little?

Watching the three talk allowed me to notice something. Doesn't it look like Mishuel has the perfect harem setup? Two beautiful girls and soul-healing beast people. I'm a vending machine, so I guess that makes me the magic item of the group.

If not for me, it might have been the ideal fantasy party.

After Lammis's moment of embarrassment, Mishuel took the chance to loosen up. He even began eating with everyone else, and by the time another week had passed, he'd gotten quite used to it.

It's delightful that he's gradually getting over his social anxiety... Mm-hmm.

"I have to say, Boxxo is a very talented magic item."

"Isn't he? His food and drinks are tasty, he gives us lots of useful tools, and he protects us with Force Field. He's great!"

Please, you're embarrassing me with all this praise! Lammis isn't saying that just because I'm nearby; she really means it, which I guess makes her who she is.

"I've personally seen many magic items, but this is the first time I've seen one like this."

"I'd bet. Far as I know, there's no magic items recorded in any literature that are like Boxxo. If he could talk, we could get information, too... but there's no point asking for the impossible."

"Still, it's amazing just that you can understand one another. Isn't it, Boxxo?"

"Welcome."

I'm glad Mishuel is receiving me so warmly, too.

Now that he's gotten closer with Lammis and Hulemy, I'm starting to get suspicious that things might evolve into love affairs, but I also can't shake the feeling that that won't be happening anytime soon.

One handsome-looking guy and two beautiful women. They paint a pretty picture, but they don't seem interested in one another. Their daily conversations are so dull that it makes me think they each have their hearts already set on other people.

Over two weeks have passed since we began our periphery investigation, but other than Lammis's physical issue, nothing out of the ordinary has happened. We're poised to make a full revolution without even running into any other creatures.

There weren't any tears or damage in the labyrinth's walls, so it looks like our quest will end as a simple safety check. By Hulemy's calculations, we should arrive at the Labyrinth stratum settlement in another three days. I'm glad this will end without incident.

I've provided them food at fairly low prices, so I haven't accrued much in the way of points, but I still have five hundred thousand or so. There's no need to rush.

The three talk cheerfully among themselves. Since he's wearing jet-black armor, a quick glance would paint him as an attractive yet imposing warrior, but when you look more closely, you'll realize Mishuel is short—he looks like a little brother accompanied by his two older sisters.

I guess our trip is going to end without any lovey-dovey developments; they just ended up becoming friends.

Come to think of it, he mentioned having an older sister, so he was probably little-brother material to begin with. It would be natural to have an interest in women at that age, but he hasn't shown a single sign of that yet.

Normally, even for someone lacking any ulterior motives, it would be natural for him to feel his eyes drawn to Lammis's prodigious bust, but that didn't happen at all.

I'm in awe of his self-control.

"Hmm? …Hold up, everyone!"

Mikenne, who was in the lead, stops walking. He bares his fangs and makes the buar cart stop.

I look and see that the other Band of Gluttons members are wearing drawn-back expressions, too, and their noses are twitching, like they're sniffing something.

"Pell, can you pick out the smell?"

"Um, it's a human smell coming from ahead of us. Really smelly. They must not towel themselves off. Four or five human men. It doesn't seem like there are any other animals or monsters. Short, can you hear them?"

"Yeah. I can't make out what they're saying, but it sounds like men's voices."

Pell seems to have a sharp sense of smell, and Short's listening ability is excellent. Mikenne nods to them as he hears what they have to say.

"Hulemy. I don't know what their goal is, but it looks like five people or so are waiting for us up ahead."

"You serious, Mikenne? Hunters on the outer perimeter…? It can't be. There's no reason to hang out in this creature-less wasteland. If we assume they're friendly, they'd be messengers from Director Bear, but…"

"Maybe an emergency came up?"

Something may have happened that suddenly required our talents. But if it was urgent, there would be more than just people on foot. Normally, they'd use a buar cart or horses—I don't know if horses exist here—but in any case, they would have some sort of way to move faster than walking pace.

Besides, if their only purpose was to tell us about something in a wasteland that contained no natural threats, they wouldn't need four or five people. This is starting to get suspicious.

"Uh, this might not be good. That many people wouldn't be coming on foot just to convey a message. Unless they get lonely easily or they're super-cautious."

Hulemy shares my opinion. If we assume they're hostile, their aim would be me, a magic item. Or perhaps they're slave traders after Lammis and Hulemy because they're pretty.

Now that I think of it, the Band of Gluttons are a rare species, and they're adorable—at least when they're quiet—so they'd probably be popular with people who dealt in exotic animals. In an illegal way, of course.

That's about all I can come up with. If they came to an empty stratum and kidnapped someone, people would assume they had died in the labyrinth, and that would be the end of it. That raises the question of what they'd do about transfer circles, but maybe there's a way to bypass them.

"I must apologize to you all. It's likely the people waiting for us are connected to me," says Mishuel bitterly, his face clouded.

Now, that's something I hadn't considered. We don't know for sure yet, but he must have a clue as to why they're after him.

"I'll face them alone. I can't cause trouble for any of you."

Mishuel snaps back into his handsome-guy mode and begins to walk off without waiting for an answer—when Lammis grabs his shoulder.

"We don't know for sure yet, do we? Besides, if it's dangerous, we can't let you go alone."

"Please, let go. If you're with me, your life will be in..."

He tries to brush her hand away, but there's no way he'll escape Lammis's iron grip on his shoulder pad. He's like a kid flailing and trying to get away from a parent.

"Oh, calm down," says Hulemy. "Are you at all willing to tell us why they might be after you?"

"No."

He flat out rejects Hulemy's question. The quick response seems to indicate he has a secret.

I wonder if it's complicated family issues. If his only secret was his social anxiety, there wouldn't be any problem—well, that *is* still a problem, but it's not as serious as whatever this other thing he's hiding is.

"I know you're concerned for our safety, but you don't need to worry," says Hulemy. "Not as long as Boxxo is with us."

"Yeah. With Boxxo by our side, we don't even have to worry about getting hurt."

They both put their absolute trust in me, so my answer is obvious.

"Welcome."

I'm confident that if they stay close, I can protect them with Force Field.

Mishuel doesn't seem convinced by our exchange, though. He stares at me with narrowed eyes, holding his tongue. Well, the facts will speak for themselves.

I wrap everything in a Force Field, including Lammis, who is carrying me right now.

"What in the world is this blue light?"

"This? It's Boxxo's Blessing, I think. Hulemy says it's called Force Field. It's an unbreakable wall that can deflect any attack. Apparently, it even blocked a stratum lord's attack."

Oh, Mishuel just frowned. He's staring closely at me, as though suspicious of what he's seeing. I guess it's only natural he can't believe it.

"You can't trust it—I get where you're coming from. As a test, try hitting it with all your might. If your attack doesn't get through at all, you'll let us come with you. How does that sound?"

"Are you sure? Will you promise not to follow me if it can't block this?"

His eyes sharpen, and I feel a tight, tense mood coming from him. I'm fully aware that Mishuel isn't saying all this because he hates us. He'll persist with his cold attitude if it means distancing us from danger.

But Lammis is a big softy who carries a vending machine. That's not enough to make her waver.

"Yup, that's okay," she says. "If that sword gets even a little bit through the Force Field, we'll stay here for the entire day. I promise."

Unfaltering in the face of his icy stare, Lammis looks him right back in the eye.

Mishuel seems to sense a strong willpower from her eyes. He unsheathes his greatsword from the giant sheath on his back. The grip has an intricate design, with an engraving that looks like a dragon's body. Above his hands gripping it is a dragon's head in place of a guard, and a translucent red blade extends from its gaping jaws. It looks like raging flames bursting from the maw of a black dragon, and it's so imposing that just seeing it is enough to make me shudder. It'll be worth using Force Field for this. I'll never let it pass through—I have to meet Lammis's expectations.

"I won't hold back. Here I go."

He shoulders the blade and lowers his posture. His stance is so cool… But now's not the time to entertain such carefree thoughts. Come on, now—whatever you hit me with, the Force Field will block it! Do your best, Force Field! You can win, Force Field!

...I get excited and cheer it on, but now I'm kind of feeling a little embarrassed at relying so heavily on the Force Field.

"Haaaaahhhhhh!"

Mishuel sharply exhales, and the red blade comes crashing down. The tip travels along a slightly sunken path, and the edge closes in on me—but by that time, it's already collided with the Force Field.

[Points decreased by 500.]

Whoa! The Force Field parried the blade completely, but I got the pop-up showing points consumed from going over the Force Field's sturdiness. The Octo Croc, *a stratum lord*, consumed an extra thousand points with its tackle, too. Does that mean Mishuel's attack was about half that tackle's power?

That's incredible. This isn't your run-of-the-mill destructive power. Now that I've endured this, I'm curious to see how many points a full-force Lammis punch would consume.

"It blocked... It blocked my Evil Dragon's Roaring Strike?" mutters Mishuel, frustrated, still taking the recoil. That attack was incredible. I never even considered he'd be able to do half the damage of a stratum lord.

"See? It'll be fine. No matter what, we won't get hurt."

"There you have it."

A promise is a promise, and Mishuel agrees to let us go with him, albeit reluctantly. We've been going on and on completely under the pretense that we're up against enemies, but even if they end up being harmless messengers, you can never be too careful.

Pursuers

With Mishuel taking the lead, Lammis follows a short distance behind with me in tow. Mikenne is with us, too. We asked the rest of the Band of Gluttons and Hulemy to keep watch over the buar cart.

Mishuel didn't tell us what kind of adversary awaited us, but even an idiot could tell from his concerned expression that it was no half-baked opponent.

"Boxxo, if it comes down to it, I'll be counting on you."

"Welcome."

To be honest, I would have preferred Lammis to wait behind as well, but Mishuel would never be able to carry me. Now that it's come to this, all I have to do is protect her with all my strength. Still, I wonder what sort of foe is lying in wait for us.

"Lammis. There are five men in total. They seem to be after Mishuel, like he said," asserted Mikenne, his nose and ears twitching. I guess he can figure all that out with just his sense of smell if we're close enough. I've started to see them faintly in the direction of our travel, but it would be tough to pick out exactly how many of them there are.

"The three in front seem quite skilled. The other two are magic users, or possibly Blessing users of one of the four elements or something similar."

Mishuel's expression and tone are now exuding hot-guy energy. It looks like he's still in the zone.

"You can sense presences, Mishuel?"

"Yes, to an extent."

It must be convenient to be able to mentally sense that people are around. I don't think a vending machine like me would ever be able to acquire that ability, but it would be funny if presence sensing was in the Blessings or features list. I'll look for one later.

Here's where the problems start. We've told Mikenne about my Blessing already, so I don't think he'll leave our side. If things come to that, then I'm sure he'll make it out with how quickly he can run away.

Still, Mishuel probably won't let me protect him. He seems to have some kind of major secret—maybe that will come to light during this incident.

As our party advances with a confident stride, the five men come into view.

One has a scar on his cheek, apparently from being cut by some blade; he wears it like a battle-hardened warrior. Looks like he's the leader. Three are in heavy gear, with full steel-colored armor, shields, and maces.

The other two hold two-handed staves with giant crystal-like stones attached to the tip, and they wear hoods low over their eyes, looking like perfect magic casters.

The three in their front line are wearing gear that you don't see very often in the Clearflow Lake stratum. That's partly because the stratum is very humid, making metal armor a poor choice. In addition, though, not many hunters opt for blunt weapons, so seeing all three of their front-line members wielding maces is unusual.

"Lord Mishuel, correct? We have come for your life."

"I thought as much. Who sent you?"

"I am sure you know without me having to say."

"You're not wrong."

I know this is indiscreet of me to say, but there's a certain atmosphere about their exchange. I've seen this kind of thing in period films before. I'd still prefer that he clearly explain what's going on instead of leaving us to draw our own conclusions.

"By the way, the beast person there and…the girl—are they allies of yours?" The scarred warrior's gaze freezes just for a moment when it comes to me. He seems to immediately decide it's not something he can understand and stops thinking about it.

"Not allies. We just accepted the same quest. Feel free to come after me, but I won't let you lay a hand on those three."

He counts me as one of them?

Lammis's cheeks loosen at Mishuel's remarks. She must be happy that he included a vending machine like me.

"I see. If you will do us the favor of offering us your head, we will promise not to lay a hand on them."

Now, there's a sketchy remark. I've never heard anyone say they wouldn't lay a hand on someone else, then actually didn't. It's a staple among staples that once they killed Mishuel, they'd kill the eyewitnesses for fear of word spreading.

"You think I'll believe you?"

"You are free to make that decision however you wish. Now, what will you do, Lord Mishuel?"

"My answer is obvious. I'll defeat the lot of you and keep you from hurting them!"

He's the ideal image of a hero. A commanding presence with the looks to back it up. If a vending machine said that, they'd snort, and that would be the end of it.

Anyway, I'll stop enjoying myself as an innocent bystander now. I have to focus so I can activate Force Field at any time.

"How noble of you. We shall scatter you and the lofty feelings in your breast across these wastes."

The enemy group readies for battle. I've experienced Mishuel's strength firsthand, but high attack power doesn't necessarily translate into skill in a fight against another person.

Lammis can overpower Captain Kerioyl with her destructive force, but when they sparred, he very easily shut her out. I remember the captain saying, "Power is only useful in combat when paired with skill," or something along those lines.

They'll be a pain to deal with, but the biggest problems are those two in the back line who look like magic users. It's common video-game knowledge that warriors don't do well against magic. I wonder if that's true in other worlds as well.

Either way, we're not obliged to wait around for them like this.

I change form into a pressure washer. Lammis seems to get the right idea immediately upon seeing my shape; she pulls the nozzle out with me still on her back and readies it.

She knows how to use this from practicing against the flame scolls, so she'll be able to without a problem. She positions the nozzle at her hip and puts a finger on the lever.

"Mishuel, leave the back to us!"

Without waiting for a response, Lammis plunges in. Mikenne, flustered, follows suit. I'm afraid of surprise attacks, so I'll expand a Force Field ahead of time.

"What's that blue thing? Take that one out first."

The two mage-looking people point their staves at us. I just thought of something... This can block magic, too, right? It's blocked flames and heat in addition to physical attacks before, so I think it will be fine... Uh, it will, right?!

Paying no mind to my inner thoughts, balls of fire and small rocks shoot from their staff tips, turning into a sideways-sweeping hail of attacks.

Lammis, who trusts me completely, rushes headlong into the torrent of flame and stone. They collide with the Force Field's translucent walls, but they all bounce off, and it doesn't allow even one shot inside.

G-great. I guess it can block magic stuff, too. L-look, it's all right. Lammis, you can rampage to your heart's content now.

With the metal box on her back, Lammis dives straight for the enemies, unafraid of their magic. And now, they're scared. They get cold feet and start to withdraw.

"Time to spray!"

After closing to not even ten feet in distance, she pulls the lever, and highly pressurized water begins to spurt from the nozzle tip.

"What?! A Blessing that can control water?!"

Even if it hits, it doesn't have enough force to do much more than sting a little, but it's more than enough to obstruct their view. Then, I switch the water to the shampoo mode from car washes. Instead of water, bubbles erupt out, covering their bodies.

"Blurgh! Wh-what?! I can't see! My eyes!"

Yeah, it does hurt when the soap gets in your eyes, doesn't it? They flail around covered in bubbles. It was already hard for them to move in their drenched, clinging robes, but now they're slipping on the detergent and making a big show of falling over.

"Oh, this is kind of fun!"

I mean, this looks just like a one-sided water-gun fight—obviously, it's fun. Mikenne is watching us enviously. This isn't a game!

Our opponents try to stage a counterattack, but I block everything with my Force Field, leading to a one-sided trampling—actually, this seems like bullying.

"What the hell are you two doing?!"

The scarred man who seems to be the leader yells at them. They're in a three-on-one battle, but Mishuel is holding his own. Even to the untrained eye, the attackers' movements are crisp, and they're clearly skilled with their weapons.

But all that isn't enough to overwhelm him. They seem impatient, but when they learn the back line is blocked off, their impatience turns to panic, and their movements lose their composure.

We're washing off the bubbles in rinse mode now, but the water mixes with the sand in the ground and covers them in mud. They were never hit by a direct attack, but their breathing is still ragged.

Mikenne charges toward them, rope in hand, and deftly ties them up. Not only that, but he covers their eyes and wraps their mouths.

"If they can't see, they can't activate any magic or Blessings in the places they want. Some Blessings are word activated, too, so I figured I'd prevent them from contacting their friends."

Mikenne seems accustomed to dealing with these kinds of opponents; he disables both of them with tact.

"Mishuel! We're done over here!"

When Lammis shouts, it cuts off the enemies' focus, and their movements clearly start to dull. Mishuel doesn't let that opening go to waste—with three swings of his greatsword, the enemies slump to their knees and fall face-first onto the ground.

"Thank you," says Mishuel. "If you hadn't helped me, things could have gotten dicey. I'm grateful for your help."

As Mishuel bows deeply, Lammis replies with a simple "No problem." Mikenne walks over to the three felled opponents, ropes in hand. He checks their pulse and their pupils, then shakes his head.

He killed them? They came to kill him, so it makes sense: It was legitimate self-defense. I understand it mentally, but my heart stirs just a little, proof that I was raised in Japan, where peace was guaranteed.

"You've disabled the other two, I see. We can question them... Thank you for that."

No passion can be felt from his eyes; they contain a cold light.

I thought nothing of it when Lammis killed monsters, and yet, I feel a little bit of fear toward him. It's so selfish of me. This is another world—if this is enough to rattle me, I won't last.

My life in the Clearflow Lake stratum was too placid and comfortable, and that might have made my perceptions naive. Maybe I should once again brace myself for what's to come.

"Would you mind calling the others? I have something I need to ask these two."

He must want to do the interrogating while we're not around. It seems like there are things involved that our presence would cause trouble for; he's telling us in a roundabout way to leave.

"Okay. We'll go get Hulemy and the others."

And Lammis is a keen girl. Without questioning him about anything, she and Mikenne turn their backs to him and begin to walk away. As I bump up and down on Lammis's back, I stare after Mishuel, but I can't read anything from a quick glimpse at his impassive face from the side.

"Mishuel must have a lot going on."

"Welcome."

"It's hard to know how deep to pry in these situations."

"Welcome."

"I know he didn't need our help, either, but I just couldn't stay quiet. Maybe I should leave a little more distance between us."

Lammis has been thinking a lot about this, too. I don't know how to answer this question myself. Some people might think it was annoying, but other people might want someone to listen.

He looks like he's afraid of getting someone involved. He isn't refusing to have anyone else there; it feels more like he's being considerate and trying not to let harm befall us.

While I ponder it, we meet up at the buar cart where Hulemy and the others are waiting, then head back to Mishuel in no particular rush.

It was about a thirty-minute round-trip, and by the time we get back, Mishuel is standing there by himself—the two magic caster–looking people are nowhere to be found. The corpses of the three men he slayed, too—vanished.

I think for a moment he let them escape, but when I look attentively at the ground, I can see faint burn marks. They sort of look human-shaped. Five of them. Which means, well, I know what happened.

"Looks like you took care of them, eh? Nice work."

"I brought the others!"

Hulemy understands what happened here, so she purposely addresses Mishuel in a lighthearted voice. Lammis gives a little wave of her hand, too. No one can sense even a hint of seriousness coming from her.

"Welcome back. I have to apologize for getting you involved in personal affairs."

"Don't worry about it," says Lammis. "Boxxo gets caught up in lots of stuff anyway—like getting kidnapped or falling through cracks in strata."

"You're not wrong," remarks Hulemy.

"Too bad."

They were the ones who took care of me in those situations.

After hearing our exchange, Mishuel's tense expression loosens just a little. "I can't reveal the details," he says, "but for certain reasons, there are people after my life. If we stay together any longer than this, it could put your lives in danger, so I will return to the settlement ahead of you all and move to a different stratum. Thank you so much for everything you've done."

"Oh, wait a second," says Lammis. "If you're a strong person with a lot on your plate, why not join the Menagerie of Fools? The captain said they were looking for people like that."

"Right, he was rambling on about stuff like that, wasn't he?" adds Hulemy. "Doesn't matter where you come from, as long as you're the real deal. He's even bragged before about how everybody in his band has *some* kind of personal baggage."

Of all things, an invitation? Come to think of it, Captain Kerioyl was certainly saying things like that. He'd probably go, "If someone's after us, we just fight them off—it'll be good training against surprise attacks" and be perfectly fine with it. He's got a lot of spunk, after all.

"The Menagerie of Fools—that famous team of hunters?"

"Yup. It's filled with interesting people. We promised to help them out once in a while, too."

"Why not forget all the tough stuff and ask them? I think it'd be a good place to gain power."

"I...see. I'll look into contacting them. Now then, so long, until we meet again."

He's been bowing very deeply, but he swiftly straightens up and begins to leave. He cuts quite the dashing figure even when saying good-bye, but I didn't miss the mutterings carried from him to me on the wind.

"The Menagerie of Fools... There's so many people I don't know there... I can't do it..."

Ahh, I guess the hurdle is still too high for him. When he's in hot-guy mode, he's quite reliable. I suppose this gap is part of his charm.

Without anyone stopping him, we wait until his back is out of sight and then resume our progression. Things would be awkward if we sped up and caught up to him, so we slow down as much as we can, with me bouncing slowly and comfortably.

When we arrive back at the settlement after taking over twice the time it normally would have, dusk has started to blanket the sky, so we decide there's no reason to hurry and spend the night at the only inn in the labyrinth.

"A lot happened, but now we can finally go back to the Clearflow Lake stratum!"

The next day, Lammis is the only one among those standing on the transfer circle who seems to be full of energy. Hulemy stifles a yawn, and the Band of Gluttons sleepily rub their eyes.

I can't blame them. It's still early in the morning when the sun has just started to rise, so it must be a rough time of day for night people and nocturnal folk.

Yesterday, we reported to the Hunters Association that we found nothing strange, and after only a quick explanation, our mission was complete. After that, people bought large quantities of items from me, making noise until late in the night, which brings us to now.

"I'm ready to relax and do some research for a while."

"What are the Band of Gluttons going to do now? I think there are a lot of jobs available in the Clearflow Lake stratum, so you'll probably be able to make enough money so you won't go hungry."

"Then let's cut loose for a while. I hope we can eat until we're full."

"I want to take a bath."

"Director Bear governs that place, after all. Nothing bad will happen to us."

Hulemy goes without saying, but the Band of Gluttons are evidently coming to live in the Clearflow Lake stratum. I'll be able to expect them as regular customers in the future, too.

It will mean leaving the Labyrinth stratum, but we'll probably never come here again. Besides, if I hadn't been caught up in the stratum fissure, I never would have fallen here from the sky.

We met new people, but Clearflow Lake is still the best place for me to relax. We've only been gone for a little under a month, but I seem to think of it quite fondly.

I want to hurry back to business in my spot in front of the Hunters Association building, catering to my beloved regulars. Everyone else is probably looking forward to it, too. Seeing their happy faces when they buy things is something I enjoy as a vending machine.

"All right, we're going home!"

Her voice was the signal for the worker to activate the transfer circle. Light rushes up from our feet to cover us, and I feel my body grow lighter, as though it's floating.

And not a moment after I feel my consciousness cut off, the light at our feet disappears to reveal completely different surroundings.

The room we were just in was less than thirty square feet and made of wood, but now we're in a giant room made of stone. Lights that look like magic items are installed on the walls in the four corners of the room, and despite a lack of windows, their magical light ensures more than enough visibility.

"It looks like we've arrived at the Clearflow Lake stratum."

So this is the kind of place they set up the Clearflow Lake transfer circle. There's a lot of people and a lot of transportation of goods, so unless they make the room big, they might run into a bunch of issues.

Lammis throws open the door, big enough to carry me through with room to spare, and exits into the hallway. Doors line up neatly to our right, and a large window adorns the left wall.

The passage is wide enough to let four or five adults walk side by side without a problem, and it secures over ten feet in height as well. Judging by the light filtering in through the window, the Clearflow Lake stratum is experiencing clear skies.

Another large set of double doors is on the end of the long passage. When we open it, we find ourselves in the first-floor hall of the Hunters Association.

No hunters are in the hall, just the Association employees.

The ladies sit on the other side of the counter in a line as usual, and when they see us... Why is one putting her hand to her mouth in surprise?

"Huh? How did Boxxo get there?"

Huh? Oh, right. I fell through the stratum split, so obviously she'd think it was weird that I returned through the transfer circle. That must be why she's surprised.

"Boxxo got pulled into a stratum split and fell into the Labyrinth stratum. We recovered him and just came back."

Hulemy explains for me right away. The worker's questions must be cleared now.

"Oh yes, the director informed me, so I'm aware of that, but..."

Huh? Wait, why is she surprised, then? If she knows that, aren't things settled?

"Mr. Boxxo, you were doing business in the settlement this morning—no, for over a week now, correct?"

"Huh?"

Huh? My thoughts overlap with the sounds Lammis and Hulemy make. Wh-what's going on? I just got back now, and I fell to the lower stratum about a month ago. Things don't add up. It's impossible, no matter how you look at it.

"W-wait a second. Boxxo has been in the Labyrinth stratum this whole time. He never came back here."

As Lammis grabs the counter with both hands and leans forward, the employee raises a hand to stop her, somehow managing to maintain her business smile. "So you say, but I saw Boxxo myself in the settlement. Right?"

"Y-yeah. I used him yesterday, too."

The employee sitting next to her nods. They don't look like they're telling a lie. But if it's true, then do we have an imposter—or a similar item?

"In other words, there's a fake Boxxo going around… This is an alarming situation."

"A fake… We have to go complain!"

Lammis seems like she's about to burst out of the place in fury, so I declare, "Too bad."

"Boxxo, why are you trying to stop me? It's an imposter. I won't allow anyone to do business pretending to be you. We have to go make a complaint and get them to stop."

She's right, but I'm extremely interested in what they have to gain by doing this. Are they trying to replace me because I was gone? Or were they just trying to imitate me to make a profit?

If it's the latter, then calling them out on it would be barking up the wrong tree. It's basic moneymaking practice to mimic other businesses. And I'm also plainly interested in how they figured out how a vending machine works.

"Calm down, Lammis. If we don't know what they're after, we shouldn't do anything careless. Let's report to Director Bear and then go scout it out together."

Hulemy has the same opinion as me. Of course, in her case, she's probably suggesting the plan out of pure academic interest.

Lammis's anger hasn't been quelled, but she reluctantly agrees, so for now, we all decide to go to Director Bear's room.

*   *   *

Life had finally caught up with Director Bear while he was out searching for me, and he has apparently been buried in paperwork ever since coming back.

"Director, can we come in?"

"Lammis? You've returned. Please come in."

Director Bear's lethargic, utterly exhausted voice reaches us from the other side of the door.

When we open it, we find Director Bear giving a disgusted stare at the piles of paperwork on his desk. He is skillfully gripping a pen with his bear paw, but I worry needlessly whether he can write letters properly.

"I was just thinking of taking a break. Boxxo, can I purchase a cold drink?"

"Welcome."

After buying a lemon tea, he sits, sinking deep into the sofa, and downs the contents in one go. It's plain to see the fatigue has built up.

"You can all take a seat as well. Could I get you to report the results of the request?"

Hulemy, as the representative, tells him of the situation at the labyrinth outskirts. And though she seems to waver for a moment, she tells him all about Mishuel, without hiding anything.

"Mishuel? I've heard he is a talented hunter, but he never joins a group. He must have some kind of important reason for it. I'll be sure to keep that in mind."

Well, one of those reasons is his social anxiety.

"Also, Director, did you know that a Boxxo imposter has appeared in the settlement?"

"An imposter? I'm sorry, I've been holed up in this room the whole time. I know little of worldly affairs."

"Apparently, there's someone like Boxxo out there, and everyone believes it's Boxxo. We were thinking of doing a little snooping. I wanted to know if we needed the Hunters Association's permission first."

"No, you can do as you please. Any other person— Well, this expression is difficult in this case, but Boxxo is a resident of the Clearflow Lake stratum. If someone is deceiving others by saying they are a resident and making a profit, we will have to punish them appropriately. I'll make it a request from the Hunters Association. I want you to find out who they really are. But I ask that you do not resort to violence. All we need is sufficient evidence to solve the problem."

"Okay, got it. I'll unmask them, for sure!"

Lammis clenches a fist. I don't think she'll do anything violent after the director specifically warned her about it, but I'm still a little worried.

An imposter... I wonder who they are. A bit—no, a considerable amount of interest is starting to well up. I decide to look to the future in anticipation of just what we may encounter.

The Imposter

The Band of Gluttons end up remaining with Director Bear while Lammis and Hulemy set out to spy on the enemy, but I want to go with them, too.

I am most interested in this imposter. I don't only want to hear about them—I want to see them directly. Nevertheless, if they carry me around in my usual vending machine state, the jig will be up the moment we step outside. The best course of action would be to hide my identity first.

Therefore, we decide that I'll change into my cardboard vending machine form and be put into a largish bag so Hulemy can carry me. That's enough of a camouflage for me, but these two are actually already in disguise.

Lammis has her hair down instead of in a side ponytail, and she's wearing a wide-brimmed hat made of a soft material. Her clothing also consists of a cardigan and a long skirt, quieting her habitually energetic aura and making her seem more like a carefully raised young lady.

"Th-this seems kind of weird, Boxxo. Does it look good?"

"Welcome." It's the exact opposite of her usual image, and combined with her bashful behavior, it makes her exorbitantly cute. Time to take another recording with my surveillance camera.

"That's a total transformation, Lammis," says Hulemy, looking at her hard.

You can barely recognize Hulemy, either. Her normally sloppily tied-back hair is in a braid hanging at her back, and she's wearing a front-peaked hat that makes her head look larger.

She has on sleeveless clothes, but the collar is a turtleneck, and you can see from the outline of her body... She's padding her chest. She's much more buxom than usual. Below that, she's wearing low-rise shorts that expose her thighs, from which her slender, fair legs extend smoothly.

The outfit makes her look active and energetic instead of frail and reclusive.

"Your clothes are really cool, Hulemy. Don't you think so, Boxxo?"

"Welcome."

"Well, I don't prefer clothes like this."

She scratches at her head in a rare instance of shyness. Her usual black coat doesn't show too much skin, so her new outfit looks refreshing and charming. Actually, if she takes off the black coat, she ends up exposing a whole lot of skin, but only a few people know that.

She was attractive to begin with, so she'd be popular if she groomed herself a little more regularly.

"All right, let's go scouting!"

"Yeah. This is a little embarrassing, but let's go."

"Welcome."

The three of us are walking through the settlement now, but I've felt eyes from both men and women on us.

The men look at us with carnal lust in their gazes, the kind they have when talking to a beautiful woman, but the women sometimes sigh in admiration, as though captivated. Both these girls are top-tier beauties, so I understand people wanting to stare at them, but these were certainly not the right disguises for scouting out the enemy.

"Hey, this was definitely the place the fake Boxxo was, right?"

"Yeah. Where is it...? Look—close to the place the Chains Restaurant used to be."

The moment I hear that, I get a bad feeling. No, it's less a feeling and more a conviction. Actually, I think I see where this is going.

If the Chains Restaurant is involved with this incident... No, I shouldn't make assumptions. The first thing we should do is gather information at the scene.

As we proceed down the main road, the number of people steadily increases. It's before noon at the moment, so normally, people would gather at the stands in front of the Hunters Association, but not many are there today. I wonder if it's because they've all started to flow this way.

Once we exit into a place where we can physically see the former site of the Chains Restaurant, the sight of a line of people jumps out at us. At the front, we can see a giant white box. That must be my imposter. I can't see its exact shape from this distance.

There must be around ten people lined up wanting to buy something. Others, close to twenty, are eating at outdoor chairs and tables.

"Let's get in line."

"Okay."

We get to the end of the line and decide to observe things until our turn comes. The imposter is standing with its back to the wall of the former Chains Restaurant. It hasn't reopened—the store is still closed down.

As we get closer, I realize something—the imposter is twice as big as me. It easily exceeds six feet, about as tall as Director Bear. Its width and depth are twice my own, too.

Its coloring and design are close to mine, but it feels like a cheap knockoff. It gives off a very homemade feeling, but they definitely made it to impersonate me.

"Looks like it's finally our turn."

I'm peeking out the very top of the bag, so I have a great view. The thing closely resembles my design, for sure. But the items it has on sale are definitely not the same.

Drinks are shown lined up on the upper portion, but the containers are completely different. All of them are glass and have cork lids stopping them. The product names are written in this world's language above the buttons, so it seems friendlier than I am in that respect.

"Looks like they've got sweet tea, water, and juice made from squeezed fruit," says Hulemy quietly, conveying the information to me. "The price is one silver coin each."

The prices are the same as my previous ones, too? The beverages are all things you can procure in this world.

"The bottom is the food. There's fried meat, pasta, and something with bread around the ingredients."

The foods are lined up on the second row, including *karaage*, a ramen rip-off, sandwiches, and something that looks like oden. They seem to have put in quite a lot of effort, but can they actually provide them in a warm state when we buy them?

"All right, let's each get one drink and one thing to eat."

Hulemy puts a silver coin into the slot. That part is mostly the same shape as mine, too. Though the silver coin enters, the switches don't light up, so it's hard to tell whether or not you can buy something yet.

"One silver coin received."

Whoa! I heard a voice from the vending machine. Wait, they can do voice recording with this world's technology? I thought Hulemy said it was being researched but that putting the idea into application was presenting difficulties.

"A voice feature? Still..."

She puts in a second silver coin.

"Two silver coins received," says the voice again.

This time, when I calm down and listen closely, I realize that the young man's voice seems too vivid to be a recording.

Hulemy, tilting her head, puts in a third coin.

"Three silver coins re— *Cough.* Received."

It coughed! Wait, is there a real person inside this vending machine?

An evil grin appears on Hulemy's face, and she reaches out with both hands, pushing both the tea and the fried meat buttons at the same time.

"Huh...?"

Now, that definitely sounded like a confused man's voice. Everything would make sense if someone's in there. Vending machine features are still too difficult for this alternate reality's technology to replicate. But if someone's inside dealing with customers, it can still exchange money and provide the products.

A drink is placed in the compartment, but the fried meat hasn't come out yet.

"Please wait a moment," says the person inside the vending

machine. If they had fried chicken ready to go, I'd think they could give it to you right away.

Over five minutes later, the product is placed into the compartment.

When she takes it out, the fried meat is on a ceramic plate with steam rising from it. He didn't just reheat it—it definitely looks like he made it from scratch.

Could the person inside the vending machine be doing the cooking? No, that can't be. The box might be bigger than I am, but there's just not enough space for an adult to cook in there.

"Then I guess I'll have the water and the pasta soup."

The water comes out right away, but the ramen rip-off seems like it takes time, too. Though it comes out faster than the fried chicken, three minutes have already passed.

This product looks like it was just cooked as well. It's impossible to put what you need to make fried chicken and ramen inside there. I wonder what the trick is.

The two girls place their items on a nearby table and begin to eat.

"Oh, this is good. It wasn't premade."

"Yeah, you're right. It's good in a regular sort of way. Wait... This flavor is like when we ate at the Chains Restaurant."

When I hear Lammis's impressions, everything clicks. The vending machine's location is the answer to everything. The imposter is doubtless someone related to the Chains Restaurant.

I'm only guessing, but the back of the vending machine is probably open, connecting to the former Chains Restaurant building. They opened up a hole in the wall to connect to the vending machine, and when they get the money, they make the food inside the building. That means everything makes sense, right?

In that case, I have to ask why they'd be doing something so bothersome. Their biggest goal is probably to steal my customers. And maybe it's also harassment directed at me, too.

A single magic item had humiliated a big chain store. It's possible they pulled out without much resistance in order to have time to put this plan into action.

"Well, let's go back. We can talk about it more in the tent."

"Okay."

We now know how the fake vending machine works and who's pulling the strings behind the scenes, so we just have to think of a countermeasure. I don't feel good about someone copying me, but to be honest, I admire their misplaced business efforts.

If I'd been broken in the Labyrinth stratum, this little stunt would have solidified their takeover. It's a good imitation, in my opinion, but not the kind of quality that would trick my regulars.

The truth is, none of my regulars was in the line of people buying things earlier, either. I'm sure their products don't taste bad, but their frank impressions are probably that they might as well eat and drink somewhere else.

The stalls and other shops saw an increase in both flavor and food quality when I helped them before, so as things stand, the Chains Restaurant wouldn't have an advantage if they challenged them to a taste-testing contest.

I feel as though we could leave them alone, and they'd decay naturally. They have to quickly make the food when it's ordered, and they have just one vending machine, meaning their turnover rate is bad, too.

I'm skeptical as to whether they're making a profit—or if they even have a proper business going.

After that, we go back to the tent the two girls live in and start discussing it. But in the end, we reach the conclusion that if I start doing my vending machine business normally, everything will work itself out.

And so, after reopening sales at my fixed spot in front of the Hunters Association the next day, word spread in a heartbeat. My regulars swarmed me all at once, and my items began flying off the shelves.

The cooks from the stalls came, too, to buy large quantities of items to replenish their ingredient stocks. From dawn to dusk, there was no end to the hordes of excited customers. After a week, when things had finally calmed down, the imposter vending machine was gone. The wall it had been placed in front of was also boarded up.

Hopefully, this will convince the Chains Restaurant to give up, but I can't help but feel like they'll meddle in our affairs again. We're probably under careful watch after this incident.

This is a matter of pride, so a major company could actually come to try to run me out of business. Still, if they lay a hand on my friends or me, all we have to do is turn the tables on them.

Eating Contest

Several days passed after the imposter incident, and as the Clearflow Lake stratum was returning to its usual state of daily affairs, I was forced to participate in another one of the meetings held by the eatery owners, whose stores had regained their customers.

"Thanks to our employment of a large number of hunters who can use earth magic, repairs have finished on approximately ninety percent of the settlement's walls."

"Wow. The Hunters Association has been working hard, too, it seems."

"As long as we get that wall finished, we'll be perfectly defended."

Munami, the usual moderator, claps her hands, and the shopkeepers follow suit in applause. After all, now they can do their jobs without worrying about outside enemies.

The reason the repairs on the outer walls proceeded faster than we thought is, as Munami explained as well, in large part due to the Hunters Association securing a great deal of people capable of using earth magic.

Before, over half the wall was just wooden stakes, and it would be embarrassing to say it could protect against much. Now, however, the settlement is surrounded by tall, thick earthen walls.

"Silence, please, everyone. It looks like the wall will be complete in two more weeks. Once our safety is secured, we can expand the settlement even more and get a large influx of people. That is why I've been thinking of holding an event, dubbed the Wall Completion Commemoration, which will be a joint effort among all the eateries."

This is thanks to the eateries on this stratum taking the Chains Restaurant incident as an opportunity to forge a pact. It's so nice that their relationship isn't hostile but cooperative.

"I'd like for the event itself to be an eating contest."

"Yeah. Hunters eat a ton, after all. They'll be excited, eh?"

"Right. And if we offer the winner a prize, we can expect a lot of participants."

"Plus, if we take a small entrance fee, we won't end up in the red because of it."

An eating contest, huh? A standard event with simple rules. This should be exciting.

"I got it. We should go with the most filling foods we can."

"Why don't we separate the women—and have them eat sweets?"

"On the other hand, if we use food that's easy to eat to show off how much they're eating, it might make the crowd happier."

Varied opinions go back and forth in an energetic debate. They relied totally on me last time, so it sets me at ease seeing them getting this pumped up about it on their own.

Well, I guess it's rude to talk like I'm somehow above them. I'm just borrowing the power of the items I can put into the vending machine anyway.

"Then let's aim to do this in two weeks and have the general store owner create flyers and posters. Let's keep the energy levels up, everyone!"

"Yeaaah!"

As I watch the store owners thrust their fists into the air, I wonder if it was really necessary for me to be here... They didn't ask for my opinion even once. I feel a bit left out.

When I look at how excited the owners are— Seriously, why did they bring me here?

◆

Several days passed after that, and the settlement is now bustling with festival preparations.

They've decided the event will take place in front of the Hunters Association building, and they're proceeding apace with the venue setup. It's still under construction, so there are more than enough carpenters—even though it'll be used for only one day, they're creating an awfully grandiose stage for this. Posters with contest information on them are hung everywhere the eye can see, and flyers are being passed out as well. It looks like we're reaching peak excitement in anticipation of the big day.

Each of the stores will apparently provide the participants with prizes; if you manage to slip into the top five, you'll get a fairly large prize. I've only heard a few possibilities being thrown around, but the weapons shop and item shop are giving away a full set of hunter's weapons and tools. The other prizes sound like things any hunter would want, too.

Because of all that, the number of willing participants in the contest increases by the day, and the organizers practically weep with joy. I'm happy for them.

"Mr. Boxxo, please, we'd like you to lend us your strength!"

I've been invited to an extra meeting again—and those cries of delight have turned into just plain crying as the store owners start whining all at once to me.

Every single person wears a tragic expression as they press into me like a horde of zombies.

"H-hey, you're scaring him!"

"Settle down a little, old-timers."

Lammis and Hulemy, who came with me, placate the store owners, who manage to calm down.

"Anyway, what do you want to ask Boxxo, exactly?" asks Hulemy. "Last I heard, preparations for the eating contest were going just fine."

"Uh-huh. I'm going to enter, too."

"About that, Lammis. You're right—it's going great, and we have more participants every day. At least, it *was* great, until we found out *they* would be competing."

Munami stops talking there and stares at Lammis with a grave look.

They, eh? From that dangerous-sounding tone, I imagine some assassin has blended in with the goal of disrupting the event. The Chains Restaurant would be a likely candidate.

Munami opens her mouth to speak again.

"That infamous contest wrecker, Shui the Inhaler, as well as the Band of Gluttons, will be taking part in the eating contest."

Suddenly, I understand the situation they've found themselves in. The biggest eater of the Menagerie of Fools has an appetite that the number of coins she's put into me can vouch for. On any given day, she can easily eat five times what a normal person can and then say, "It's easier to move around when you're not full" with a completely straight face. If she's competing, I can't blame the store owners for being so rattled.

And the four from the Band of Gluttons are participating with her? Their stomachs are nothing to scoff at. Once before, when all five were eating and drinking for real, they made me have to restock my items twice.

Apparently, it's possible for Tasmanian devils to eat half their weight in food in a single sitting. Despite being small, they must weigh around fifty kilograms. In that case, if they pulled out all the stops, they'd easily be able to eat over twenty kilos. And if four are participating, I really can't blame these guys for falling into despair. Nope.

They will be charging a small entrance fee, but that's not going to be anywhere near enough when it comes to those five.

"At this rate, we won't just take a loss—we'll go bankrupt! No amount of our cooking will be enough!"

"I heard that eating contests the Band of Gluttons enter don't just run out of food—they run out of garbage, too…"

"We put all this effort into joining forces, but now we're doomed!"

Heartbroken, the store owners pound their fists on the ground, but they don't forget to spare a flattering glance or two for me. I remember this exact thing happening once before. Just quit it with this little farce for now.

"Okay, I see. You want Boxxo to suggest ways or products that will do something about those five big eaters, right?"

Appearing to have learned from previous experience, the owners nod in time with one another. They started at the exact same moment, and they nodded the same number of times. I want to believe it's all coincidence.

In order to satisfy those big eaters, we have to either feed them a lot—or have them consume something filling beforehand or during the event.

I know— Why not make their drinks carbonated? If they make the contest foods heavy or spicy, they'll get thirsty more easily and have more of the carbonated drinks.

The meal would have some problems in the health area, but for an eating contest, health doesn't matter one bit.

With that settled, I drop a two-liter bottle of cola into my compartment. Lammis takes it and places it on the table. The store owners all gather around, but they're confused as to what it is.

"Um, this is a fizzy drink that feels funny when it goes down your throat," explains Lammis.

"I drink it because I like it," adds Hulemy, "but it's sweet and fills you up fast. I think Boxxo wants to say that if he provides this along with the food, it might reduce the amount of food they eat. Right, Boxxo?"

"Welcome."

They don't seem to grasp it even after hearing their explanation, so Lammis pours some into cups for everyone. They take it, but again, they just look at it; nobody puts it to their lips.

Every time it bubbles, they give a start. Unable to watch them continue like that, Hulemy downs hers in one gulp.

"Phew! I could get addicted to the way it bubbles down my throat."

Seeing her drink it enthusiastically and wipe her mouth seems to whet their curiosity, and they all drink, though only a sip.

"Whoa, what is this? I've never felt anything like this before."

"It's like something's popping in my mouth. It might be too sweet, but it goes down easily, thanks to how fizzy it is."

"I think I like this."

It looks like they have mostly good opinions of it. Still, some people might not enjoy it, which could be a problem.

"If we served this instead of water, wouldn't the participants complain?"

"Ahh, yeah. I'm not sure I can drink much more of this."

"In that case, why not let them choose between this or water?"

"No, if we do that, the ones who pick water will have a clear advantage."

At this point, I have to leave it to the owners. In complete contrast to before, they offer one insight and proposal after another, so I'd like to think they'll be fine now.

I remain an observer for a while, and as Lammis and Hulemy sip their milk tea, also not saying anything, the organizers come to a decision.

The eating contest will offer both water and cola, and they'll leave it up to the contestants to pick which one they want. In doing so, those who choose water will have a clear advantage, but they thought of an interesting way around that.

In the days leading up to the contest, the stores will all stock cola, selling small amounts for rather high prices. By doing that, when the contestants learn they can have the cola for free at the eating contest, many might be swayed to choose the cola instead.

Why, that's brilliant. If you really want to try to win, you should pick the water, but they're not in the eating contest as a job. I wouldn't blame them for losing to the temptation right in front of them.

"There you have it, Mr. Boxxo. If you could provide it to us at a reasonable price, we would be greatly in your debt."

As the store owners rub their hands and make their request, I almost give them an exasperated grin. But I'd planned to sell it to them at a price that wouldn't drive them into the red from the start, so I accept with a "Welcome."

Now the preparations are complete. All that's left is to wait eagerly for the day of the contest.

The Day of the Eating Contest

Wow, the place is packed. With clear skies overhead, crowds line up in order to get participation certificates for the eating contest. They're old, young, male, and female, of many races, showing the fruits of the publicity until now.

In the end, they decided on fried meat as the eating-contest food, but there were way more participants than we had anticipated, so they apparently mobilized all the hunters to gather ingredients.

In the kitchen set up behind the venue, there are piles of meat so high one might worry that the creatures who made their habitat near the settlement had been hunted nearly to extinction.

Come to think of it, the guy in charge of the cooking was saying something strange earlier. What was it again…?

"Agh, there's not enough meat. What now? It looks like we hunted most of the creatures nearby. Meat, meat, me— Wait, I know just the thing. They brought it back home with them after their last hunting quest."

Wait, does that mean it's frog-fiend or crocodile-fiend meat…? Oh, wait, it's common practice to eat monster meat in this world. I shouldn't try to shove Japanese ethical views onto these people, nope.

After one thing or another, it looks like they got ahold of more than enough meat. Right now, they're asking contestants before the event whether they'd like cola or water, and just as they schemed, a lot of people seem to want the cola.

The problem children—Shui the Inhaler and the Band of Gluttons—seem to have taken a liking to the cola as well, so I guess that means we've cleared the first hurdle.

"Boxxo, you'll be providing drinks during the whole eating contest, right?"

"Welcome."

That's right—my job is to replenish their cola supplies, which have grown thin on the edge of the stage. We have over fifty participants, so the fried meat is one thing, but the cola consumption will likely be significant.

Lammis suggested we should season the fried meat more heavily as well, which is sure to double the rate at which they'll get thirsty.

"Okay. I have to go through the line, so I'll set you on the stage for now."

"Welcome."

She puts me on the edge of the stage, but it's still a fairly conspicuous position.

In this settlement, there is interest in me, a vending machine, being here, but more than a few people are too scared to approach me, so one of this event's other goals is to make an appeal to my usefulness and safety. At least, that's what Director Bear said.

The stage is on a raised platform, so I can look out across the audience and the surroundings. And boy, is there still a long line in front of the person giving out participation certificates.

Lammis is near the end of the line, with the Band of Gluttons grouped up in front of her. It also seems that Shui isn't the only one participating from the Menagerie of Fools—the red-and-white twins are as well.

I know several of the other participants, too. The two gatekeepers are competing? Gocguy, from the money-changing business, is evidently participating as well. With a muscular build like an inverted triangle, he looks like a big eater indeed. You could probably add him to the list of potential champions.

My early-morning regulars have taken their seats in the audience.

Scanning them quickly, I can spot other customers who make frequent use of me here and there.

The audience's eyes are focused on me for some reason. There seem to be two groups: Some are watching me with curious eyes, and others are staring dubiously, wondering why I'm here.

As I sit in an unbearable situation, they're getting the venue equipment in order, and it looks like they've already placed all the chairs and tables. They have long tables connected to one another on the stage, with over twenty chairs in position.

After they finish setting up, Munami, the moderator and emcee, proceeds onto the stage. She's wearing her usual maid-style apron skirt. Come to think of it, I've never seen her wear anything else.

"Thank you for waiting, everyone. We will now begin the first Clearflow Lake Stratum Eating Contest!"

Clapping and cheering rise from the audience. The seats are nearly filled to capacity. Most of them have brought items they purchased from nearby vendors to come and watch.

Watching an eating contest on an empty stomach is like torture, after all. Look at this—the stalls can expect substantial earnings today.

"We have more participants than expected, so we will be splitting them up into Group One and Two. The top five from each group will advance to the finals, where we'll have one last contest. We have some incredible prizes for the winners, too, so please do your best, everyone."

"Yeeeaaahhh!"

Deep voices shout from near the bottom of the venue. The participants' excitement is reaching its peak, too.

"Then may I please have those in Group One come to the stage?"

As large men file in, the four from the Band of Gluttons appear, too. Shui and Lammis must be in Two—I don't see them among the contestants. Actually, it feels rather messy with just men.

At a glance, one man, over six feet tall and incredibly rotund, looks like a fierce competitor. But I'm very familiar with the Band of Gluttons's voracious appetites, so I wonder if he can beat them.

"The contest will last as long as the sand takes to fall through this hourglass."

A giant hourglass is placed on the stage directly opposite me. They must be using it in place of a stopwatch. I guess even other worlds have hourglasses.

Large plates stacked with fried meat are placed in front of the contestants. With that much, it's easily over two kilograms.

"Of course, those who finish their food before time runs out will automatically advance to the finals. Now, are you all ready? Then let the eating contest begin!"

All at once, the participants begin throwing steaming-hot fried meat into their mouths.

"Hot, hot!"

"Fuuu-fuuu…"

They're right out of the fryers, so the juices probably came out inside their mouths. The big men have their hands over their mouths, writhing. Quite a few of them drink the cola poured into their jugs to neutralize the heat, too.

More importantly, the Band of Gluttons… They're bringing the food to their mouths, then blowing on it. Animals' tongues tend to be particularly heat sensitive. Their pace probably won't improve until it cools down. Rude though it may be, their desperate attempts to eat through the pain warm my heart.

They're getting the food down by cooling it with the cola, but if they do that, the carbonation will probably fill their stomachs in a heartbeat. I wonder if they'll be okay. Ah, right, for the project planners, maybe it would be better if the Band of Gluttons dropped out now. I'm fairly conflicted on the issue.

The Band of Gluttons are profitable customers of mine, and we're linked by fate in one way or another, so personally, I want them to do well.

This is the first of the various strategies the store owners came up with: the piping-hot-food plan. With everyone guzzling the cola, it seems to have worked. As a bonus, the owners are buying chilled colas from me, one after another.

I look at the hourglass and see that half the sand is already on the bottom. Some will probably finish eating soon.

"I'm done eating!"

"I'm finished, too."

"Me too!"

"All done over here."

The Band of Gluttons all pump their hands in the air nearly at the same time. I expected this, but still, all four made it through? The shop owners are giving them polite applause, but on closer inspection, I can see their uncomfortable grimaces behind their smiles.

They're probably cursing their luck that four of the most problematic contestants made it to the next round. I hope they have enough food for the finals…

"I have finished eating as well."

Oh, Gocguy finished, too? That's all five of the people advancing. That was faster than I thought. Wait, only one human actually made it out of Group One. The Band of Gluttons sure are incredible.

"We have our five winners in advance of the time limit. The rest of you may feel free to bring your food back with you. We'll provide containers as well."

That's very nice of them, considering it's an eating contest. Some of the participants were in the middle of eating, but they begin to pack their food into containers and leave the stage.

When everyone from Group One is gone, people come in to clean up the leftovers and plates. In a matter of minutes, they're done preparing for the next group.

"Now it's time for the Group-Two contestants to take the stage for the eating contest!"

The line of people appearing on the stage has a high ratio of women, unlike Group One. Shui, one of the favorites, is there, of course, but Lammis is, too. My partner waves energetically as she comes onstage.

Lammis, in contrast to her physique, is a big eater, too, but I don't think she can win if pitted against Shui. Moreover, a few female hunters are participating as well. I'm usually in front of the Hunters Association, so I've memorized the faces of many hunters who come and go.

Wait, Shirley is competing, too? She certainly doesn't give the impression that she's a big eater. She seems to have realized her dress wouldn't fit the situation, and while her outfit is somewhat rougher

than usual, it's as revealing as ever. The men in the audience are getting lively.

Maybe Two had so many women to add color to the finals. The Band
of Gluttons, ever the adorable bunch, were in Group One, giving the
contest a good balance.

"Okay, Group Two, dig in!"

At the announcement, the participants begin wolfing down their
fried meat. Just like before, the fresh heat takes many of them off guard,
making them wash it down with cola.

Shui has always liked drinking cola; she drinks it calmly while happily cramming her mouth with fried meat. One thing that adds to her
appeal is how happy she looks when she eats something tasty. She puts
a hand to her cheek in an expression of bliss as she chews heartily.

The pile of meat in front of her depletes with each passing moment.
At first, it seems like Shui is taking big bites but not chewing very much,
but if you watch closely, her jaw and cheeks are blurring up and down
at high speed. She's properly chewing her food… Her speed just greatly
outpaces the other contestants'.

As though she's eating at several times the speed of those around
her, her amount of fried meat decreases rapidly. Despite her swift eating, though, that contented smile remains on her face. How wonderful.

When Shui eats, she consistently wears a smile, always looking like
she's never been happier. That's why I like her.

"Whoa… Those pouch-panda fiends are famous for being big eaters,
but how crazy is that girl over there?"

"Is she even human…?"

The astonished voices from the crowd are referring to the way
Shui eats.

"Thanks for the food!"

Before the hourglass even reaches the halfway point, Shui finishes
eating, then downs the rest of her cola in one gulp. The Band of Gluttons
were fast, too, but if we're being honest, I knew she'd win.

"I've finished eating, too."

The next one to calmly raise her hand is a woman in black-rimmed
spectacles wearing what looks like a suit—it's the money changer,

Acowi, of all people. Whether it's her or Shui, I bet a lot of women envy them for being such big eaters despite how skinny they are.

The next to advance came a good while after that.

"I... I'm done eating. It was so yummy."

Lammis rubs her belly; seems like she managed to finish. The remaining two people finish up as well, but I've never seen them before. They might be newcomers who came to the stratum recently and don't go near the Hunters Association building very much.

Incidentally, Shirley continued to eat elegantly until the end. Well, the crowd loved her, so that alone made it worth participating.

"We now have all our finalists! The finals will take place in two hours, so please wait until then. Once we're done cleaning the stage, a theater group will be performing a play. Please get your food and drinks from the stalls and enjoy."

They're having a play? They're more serious about this event than I thought. I've never once heard of a theater troupe in this settlement... Does that mean they hired them for the eating contest?

"Boxxo, I'll take you off the stage. You'll get in the way of the play."

"Welcome."

If there was a vending machine onstage while actors were doing their best to perform, it wouldn't matter what the play was about—it would just seem strange. I'll let her carry me off without complaint.

"Do you want to watch the play, Boxxo?"

Hmm, should I? I'm interested in plays, but I've never been suited to watching theater. It's not like TV, so I always worry that the actors will mess up. I know it's none of my business, but it keeps me in such suspense that I can't think about the actual play.

Back when I was little, I once went to a superhero show for kids. An unexpected event happened there that resulted in one of the costumed people getting exposed, and it all turned into chaos. I think that's the root cause of this tendency I have.

Ahh, but I still want to know what it's like. Theater troupes must be proficient, since there's so little entertainment in this other world, so they probably rarely mess up. It'll be fine.

"Welcome."

"You're interested? Okay, let's watch it together."

"Oh, you two gonna watch the play? Lemme join ya."

Hulemy came, too. I look over in the direction of her voice and see her wearing her usual black coat, hands full of food from the stalls. How nice that she seems to be fully enjoying the festival.

"Lammis, want something?"

"No way. My stomach feels like it's going to explode!"

Can't expect much from her in the finals in two hours, huh? It makes sense, given how much fried meat she ate. I guess this is where I should actually praise her for doing so well.

The audience seating is 70 percent full, but the corner of the back row is free, so we decide to sit there. I have to be on the end or else people behind us won't be able to see, so we need to be careful choosing seats, too. After all, it's awful sitting with a tall person in front of you at the movie theater.

So a play in another world, huh? I wonder what the quality will be like. This world has no TV or movies, so maybe this is a polished art. On the other hand, since people aren't used to watching theater, they might like it even if the actors are bad.

Whatever the case, for now, I'm going to sit back and enjoy this play in another world.

The Victor and the Reward

Preparations for the play look finished, so I'll sit up straight—although, with my spine, er, *body*, always positioned completely upright, I should be fine.

I'll just stand here quietly so I don't interfere with the performance.

"Why, if it ain't Boxxo. What are you doing over here?"

"I'll have some cold tea today."

But I didn't think the pair of gatekeepers would arrive at that exact moment.

With the play about to start, I don't want to make noise, so I'll show off a silencing effect using the item-dropping technique I've mastered.

With the gentleness of a mother laying her baby down in a crib, I quietly place the items in my compartment.

Great, it made almost no noise. People—well, vending machines—can do it if they try.

"What was on the program again?"

"Um, I think it was…"

Wait, are Karios and Gorth here to see the play, too?

Keeping our voices down so we don't disturb others and trading impressions could be fun. Personally, I'm all for it.

"According to the schedule they passed out before…it's apparently called *The Farm That Calls Happiness*. Never heard of it."

What's a farm that calls happiness? I can't even begin to guess. If even the well-informed Hulemy doesn't know what it is, does that make it some obscure story or a complete original?

The tale will probably be about a farm. A beautiful girl working her hardest to cultivate the fields, passing out the vegetables she raises, and making everyone happy—something like that.

I would have preferred a more otherworld-like sensational action movie. If there's a romance involved, I'm not confident I'll keep watching. Maybe I shouldn't get my hopes up too much.

"Well, we'll know when we see it. Oh—looks like it's starting."

You're right. There's no point thinking about what it will be before seeing it. Time to enjoy it as just another member of the audience.

"That was, well, unexpected in a lot of ways…"

"So they did that, and then that happened…"

"Yup, it was definitely a farm that called happiness. Oh, but it didn't really call it, it just kind of came to it…"

Everyone trades various impressions, amazement plain on their faces.

My honest opinion is that it was impressively otherworld-like. That sums it up. I can't believe the main character wasn't a person but the farm. My general view is that it was interesting, but it wasn't for everyone.

The performance was high quality, too, so if the same troupe does a different play sometime, I'd like to see it.

"Wait, this is no time for being flabbergasted. Lammis, you're in the finals, right?"

"Oh, that's right! Boxxo, let's go!"

"Welcome."

Lammis bounces me onto her back and carries me away.

"Do your best, Lammis! We're rooting for you!"

"Don't overdo it."

"Show them a woman's pride!"

As the three send words of support after her, Lammis raises a fist in the air. Unfortunately, she's carrying a vending machine, so she can't see Hulemy and the others.

With a breakaway sprint, she places me on the stage's corner, then runs off to where the contestants are waiting. I get that she's in a hurry, but she needs to be careful she doesn't trip in her haste.

"Ahh, I-I'm sorry!"

A crash and a cry reach me, but I'll pretend I didn't hear.

The stage preparations finish, and the emcee, Munami, steps out once again.

It looks like the finals are about to begin. The audience seats are only about 60 percent full, which is a little on the empty side. Maybe the first half of the contest was satisfying enough for a lot of people.

I'd like things to be more exciting to attract more people. Do I have any way to gather people here? Isn't there anything I can do? It would be nice if there was a useful feature for it.

I scan the list of additional features I got after becoming Rank 2, then spot an interesting one. If I use it, it should draw people in *and* get the place excited.

From my features list, I choose Jukebox and activate it.

"Now, will the contestants enter the stage?"

Most of the audience is paying attention to emcee Munami, so nobody seems to notice my quiet change.

I grow smaller than my usual vending machine form, and my edges take on a familiar roundness. Two thick, plastic, fluorescent light–like things are installed on my body's framework, which shine with a yellow light. Inside me, I can feel several hundred records in place of my usual food and beverages.

You used to be able to find this machine in cafés and bars, and you could put a coin in to listen to your favorite song. For anyone in their twenties to their forties, though, the jukeboxes in bowling alleys where you can play brand-new songs are probably more familiar.

By the way, jukeboxes are perfectly fine vending machines, but most people probably don't think of them that way. Of course, as a vending machine maniac, every time I'd see one I'd have it play something for me.

The reason I purposely chose an old type rather than a brand-new model is because it's full of classic music.

"Huh? Where's this song coming from?"

The audience fortunately seems to think it's part of the show, but Munami and the other organizers are at a loss. Still, Munami pushes forward without panicking or making a fuss, impressing me with her composure.

I cast my worries to the wind and decide to provide some acoustics. Munami's coping skills must have been honed by real-life events.

"Is everyone excited?! This is the end, whether it makes you cry or smile. All the participants, please eat your hearts out!"

Pumped up by the background music, Munami is bursting with energy. In that case, in order to not fall behind, I'll chose an exciting song with a faster tempo.

"The finals will be decided by how much you can eat within the time limit! Surpass your limits and open the door to a new world... Let the finals begin!"

As she makes her announcement, I change the song. I play one often heard for the relay race or footraces at sports days. Whenever I hear it, it really lifts my emotions. It looks like the contestants are eating quite a bit faster, too.

I do feel like I overexcited them a little, but there are people standing by with healing-type magic and Blessings, so the absolute worst won't happen.

It's still only just begun, but as expected, the vacuum girl, Shui, and the Band of Gluttons have jumped out ahead right from the start. Lammis doesn't have the same momentum as before—she seems to be enjoying her food at a slower pace.

The fried meat lined up in front of the five potential champions continues to be gulped down like air. The culinary spectacle of multiple pieces disappearing every second is in its own dimension at this point. That contest area is turning into a small black hole.

"Yeaaahhh! Keep it up, short-haired girl!"

"You can do it, Gluttons!"

Impassioned shouts of support fly at Shui and the Band of Gluttons. I get it—watching how they eat makes you want to cheer them on.

The other members seem to understand they can't beat those five, but they keep eating, not wanting to be outdone. Once the five put down the fried meat, the next course consists of crepes so gigantic you could easily wrap a baby in one.

For the finals, the plan was to serve a mountain of fried meat first and then have giant crepes waiting for anyone who managed to finish. A sweet follow-up attack when your stomach is already bulging. I think this contest is made to break both your stomach and your mind.

Incidentally, the crepes are stuffed to a ridiculous degree with apples and bananas I provided. To give them apples, I turned into an apple vending machine, and for bananas, a banana-specific vending machine. They're both items I enjoyed purchasing in my former life.

There is a fruit version of the vegetable vending machine, too, but I want you to understand that there's no way I wasn't going to go for the more specific ones.

By the way, I found the apple vending machines on the second floor of New Osaka Station. Not only did they have sliced apples; there were versions for chocolate-, honey-, and caramel-covered ones, too. I remember being delighted at the wide variety.

The men competing take one look at the giant crepes and make a face, but the women's eyes light up.

"Ngh—sweets! And they look mighty tasty, too!"

Lammis, you're slipping into your accent.

"May we have them as well?" Next to her, I swear I see Acowi's eyes glimmer, deep behind her glasses.

You may be wondering why the women are overreacting to something so sweet. One part of it is that many women enjoy sweet foods to begin with, but it's also because sugar and fruit are precious in this world.

This stratum can provide sweet things for cheap (thanks to me), and it seems like paradise for women and certain men who enjoy sweet foods. I've even heard a rumor that recently, some laborers and hunters came to stay in Clearflow Lake for work because they had their eyes on that.

Lammis's and Acowi's eating speeds visibly increase. At this rate, they should be able to finish the fried meat.

Shui has cream stuck all over her mouth as she devours the crepes with a full smile. Is she going even harder than she was with the fried meat...? Her nickname, the Inhaler, is no joke. Wow, she's already tripled her speed.

"That girl is nutso. And she looks like she loves the damn stuff."

"Just watching her is making me hungry. I'll go grab something from a stall."

"Get something for me, too. I want meat and sweets!"

Incited by Shui, many of those in the audience buy some extra food. It's only natural that seeing someone eat so happily would whet your appetite.

Oh, and as for the current situation: The males in the Band of Gluttons have opened their crepes and are eating the fruit out of the inside first. The lone female in their group, Suco, is just gobbling them down normally, though.

At this pace, it'll be a one-on-one between Shui and Suco. I check the hourglass; about 70 percent of the sand is gone. The men are essentially destroyed, and even the males in the Band of Gluttons are struggling with the cream and the crepe dough.

Ah, Lammis and Acowi have finished off the fried meat. Now they're enjoying the crepes with blissful expressions. They've completely put the contest aside and moved into their after-meal teatime.

From what it looks like, Shui and Suco are evenly matched. If they keep going like this, they might even finish the giant crepes before time is up.

With the organizers' fervent gazes upon them, one fork-holding hand flies valiantly into the air before all the sand in the hourglass falls.

"Yeah, I'm finished!"

With cream all over her mouth, Shui grins in satisfaction. It's nothing short of incredible.

The amount of food that disappeared into her stomach seemed like over half her body's volume, but I'll chalk that up to the secrets of a woman's body. It'll be my loss if I think about it too deeply.

"Yeaaaaahhhhh! You're really somethin', miss!"

"You beat the Band of Gluttons?! Congratulations!"

The audience seems to be satisfied with the results, and with food in their hands, they all deliver an unabashed round of applause and cheer.

Shui of the Menagerie of Fools has clinched the eating-contest victory.

The competition ends safely with zero incidents and plenty of good vibes. The top three have gotten onto the winners' stand, and they're about to be handed their prizes.

First place is Shui. Second is Suco. And one man, Gocguy, slid into third place.

Gocguy... He didn't make a show of it at all, but he was a surprising dark horse.

I've reverted to my usual vending machine form because of my time restriction to watch them, but then...

"The winner's prize is the right to use Mr. Boxxo freely for an entire day!"

...Munami says something crazy.

I'm sorry? Wait, what was that?

Munami sneaks up to me in my confusion, brings her mouth near me, and whispers. "You *did* say you'd help in any way you could when it came to the prizes, didn't you?"

I'd like to pretend I don't remember it, but... Thinking back, I do recall agreeing to something I wasn't fully listening to. Ah, yeah, I did say that, huh? But now is the time to feign ignorance!

"Too ba—"

"No playing dumb at this point."

Urgh, she talked over me. But, well, I guess one day it will be fine. She may be a heavy eater, but even if she's after my items, she knows how expensive they are.

Was I rash? I'm a little worried, but promises are promises. No matter how much she eats, her stomach does have a limit.

There's nothing to think so deeply about, and so I accept it lightly... but little did I know, I'd end up regretting my decision...

...Nah, I'm just kidding. The truth is, I've always wanted to say a cool line like that, but I doubt there will be a problem.

The Origin Stratum

"Anyway, that means Boxxo belongs to me for the day!"

I do, indeed. Please be gentle.

The day after the eating contest, as promised, I'll be rented out to Shui for the whole day, but the place I was brought to early in the morning was...the tent the Menagerie of Fools were using as a base.

Which reminds me. After the eating contest, the eatery shopkeepers and organizers profusely apologized to me, saying they'd gotten too excited and forced me to be the prize because the idea made perfect sense at the time.

They said they'd cover all of today's expenses, but I politely refused. It was my fault for not properly listening to them and giving a half-baked reply.

"Oh man. I'm so jealous of you, Shui! Aren't you, Red?"

"You get to eat and drink as much as you want?! That's not fair, is it, White?"

The red-and-white twins stare at Shui with great envy. Shui makes no attempt to cut back on her boasting.

"Nice job, Shui. If it's for a whole day, we could go monster hunting, too."

"Indeed, Captain. Or we could possibly bring Mr. Boxxo with us for negotiations and use his rarity to convince—"

"Captain, Vice Captain, Boxxo is mine, got it? You can't borrow him."
You're not interested at all in Captain Kerioyl or Vice Captain Filmina's suggestions?

"Boxxo and I are going on a li'l date to the Origin stratum."
Wait, we are? This is the first I've heard of it. Where is the Origin stratum anyway?

"Taking him to the first stratum, are you? That place is... I get it. Guess we can't talk you out of it, then. Boxxo is bound by a promise to help us out, after all. I'll give up this time."

"That's more like it. He was supposed to be all mine today to begin with."

"Just so we're clear, Shui. Not that this would ever happen, but if you take Boxxo and skip town or sell him off, there will be consequences. We're the Menagerie of Fools, and we observe our agreement not to betray other Fools. That's our commandment."

Captain Kerioyl's eyes narrow quietly, and his voice takes on a grim quality. Looking closely, I see that the amiable expressions have vanished from all the others, their coldly lit eyes directed at Shui.

Usually, they seem to give off a roguish impression, but it feels like the air has gotten rather heavy. Not that it isn't like them, though—this could be what they're actually like.

"I gotcha, Captain. I was there when you finished off that bozo. I'd never betray another Fool."

Shui's eyes sharpen, and she says something disturbing. They look like a carefree, relaxed group, but they seem to have strict rules.

"That's right, you were. Anyway, go have some fun for the day. And don't forget to bring back some souvenirs for us. We'll be looking forward to them."

"In that case, I'd like some of that fizzy drink and stew!"
"Uhhh, then I want the fried putetu treats and some cold sweet tea!"
"Yellow soup for me, please."
"Okay! If I remember all that, I'll bring 'em back."

Shui, finished with her report and her bragging, moves to the tent's entrance. Then she turns back to me, grins, and gives a light bow.

"So, Boxxo, Lammis, you two mind tagging along for the day?"

"That's fine. Boxxo and I are like the same person in mind and body."

"Welcome."

I can't move much on my own, so out of necessity, Lammis and I are a package deal.

I didn't want to be a burden on Shui, so I initially considered putting wheels underneath myself so that she could move me around more easily, but she gave up on that idea before even going fifteen feet.

She may be a hunter, but pushing a vending machine is heavy labor for one woman, so we eventually settled on Lammis helping. If I had some legs, I could move under my own power... But if a vending machine sprouted legs and started moving itself around, it would be more than a little weird. The visuals are just too awful to imagine.

"We'll be back soon!"

That was how my day with Shui and Lammis began.

We step onto the transfer circle in the Hunters Association, and I experience teleportation for the second time. The sense of weightlessness reminds me of a roller coaster. I just can't get used to it.

When the glowing lights beneath us finally dissipate, we see that we're in a stone room, not much different from the transfer circle room in the Clearflow Lake stratum.

Upon opening the door, we find ourselves outside—apparently, it was a little hut built just for the circle.

At first glance, the place seems a bit strange. It's not very well lit. Actually, there's a stone ceiling above, and not a hint of sunlight shines through it. It must be thirty feet high.

It would make sense if the place was pitch-black, but torches and magic items are shining all over the settlement, providing more than enough visibility.

I take a look around. Houses of wood and stone line the street, and there's a lot of foot traffic. Their population density seems easily higher than Clearflow Lake's.

"I haven't been to the Origin stratum in a long time! Oh, this takes me back."

"I come here all the time."

In contrast to Lammis, who is a little fidgety, Shui gives a gentle smile. Right now, she seems quite different from the girl whose interests usually involve her appetite.

She seems to have a destination in mind, and we proceed down the major road at a quick, purposeful pace. Lammis's head bobs back and forth as she tries to take in the town while keeping pace with Shui.

When I look at our surroundings, it occurs to me that we're in a giant cave filled with houses, and the settlement feels like it was forced together. Like a village people created inside a dungeon by force... Or maybe this is what settlements are supposed to look like inside a dungeon.

The Clearflow Lake and the Labyrinth strata are technically the anomalies. Normally, you'd expect to see rocky ceilings and walls. It's a dungeon, so natural light wouldn't make it this far in. I've been too heavily influenced by the previous strata, and now my sense of normalcy is crumbling.

"Shui, where were you planning on going?"

"A bit farther down, where a bunch of people tend to gather."

That's all she says. After that, she simply walks in silence.

A place where poor people gather? I wonder if it's like a slum. It's a plain fact that such places have poor security. I don't think she is leading us into a trap, but it's better to be safe than sorry, so I'll be on the lookout. I have to make sure Lammis doesn't get hurt, at the very least.

The buildings near the transfer circle were solidly built, but around here, it's all shacks and hovels—no, things on the verge of ruin that I'd hesitate to even call houses.

With Lammis's Might, a light poke would probably be enough to reduce one to rubble.

"Okay, we're here," says Shui, turning around.

Behind her is an old wreck of a mansion. It's a single-story building with a stone wall that's over half collapsed. For a moment, it looks like it's gone uninhabited for many years, but there are signs of repairs in places.

There are no weeds growing in the yard, either. Clearly, someone has been tending to it.

"I'm home, everyone!"

Shui shouts in the direction of the mansion. A moment later, the double doors fly open, and an avalanche of children spills out. Their ages range from about two on the lower end to over ten on the higher end. There are easily more than ten in all.

"I knew it; it's Shui!"

"Welcome back! Did you bring presents?!"

"Shui, play with me, play with me!"

Within moments, Shui is surrounded by children tugging at her sleeves. The sight of them all smiling is an instant indicator of how attached they are to her.

"I'm back. It looks like everyone's doing well. That makes me happy. You'll have to wait a little before we can play. Where's Miss Director?"

"She was cleaning! Miss Director! Shui is home!"

"Yes, yes, I can hear you. Welcome home, Shui."

Appearing shortly after the children is a somewhat skinny woman. Given the wrinkles near her mouth and eyes, she's probably in her fifties or so. She has a calm smile that exudes warmth and friendliness as she pats the heads of the children who run over to her.

She's wearing a white cowl and a loose, navy-blue robe-like garment. The outfit makes her look like a nun.

"I'm home, Miss Director."

"Welcome back, Shui. Is the person behind you with the large item on her back a friend of yours?"

"Yeah, pretty much. I know her from work."

"Oh, I see. Well, you are most welcome here. Please, come inside so we can sit and chat."

"Okay, thanks— Wait, can Boxxo come in, too?" wonders Lammis.

Ah, the floor looks old, so I get the feeling I'll fall right through it. I should make doubly sure nothing happens and get her to set me up outside.

"Too bad."

"I didn't think so… Okay, I'll leave Boxxo at the entrance. Um, please wait a moment, Miss Director. Come over here, children!"

After setting me down, she turns back to the children and beckons to them. They seem confused, but Shui waves them over as well, which sets them at ease. They run to us.

I know what she wants to do, so I quickly line up some items.

"This box is magic, guys!" says Shui. "If you see something inside that you want, you can push on this bump. I have unlimited access to him for the whole day, so there's no need to hold back."

"What's this round thing?"

"That's a can with sweet fruit juice in it. But I like this fizzy black kind."

"What about this? What's this?"

"That's a snack. It's a little salty, but it's really good."

She happily explains everything, and the children grab the fallen items in delight. As a vending machine, seeing children happily enjoy my products warms my heart so much that I just have to give stuff away for free.

After making sure everyone has their drinks, snacks, and food, I change forms. My body turns mainly yellow, and inside me, uninflated balloons of various colors appear. This is a surefire way to make kids happy.

"Huh? What's this? What are these?"

Oh, the children are looking inside. Then, I begin to pump in gas and inflate the balloons. The kids take a step back in surprise, but their curiosity still wins out, and they stare quietly and excitedly at the balloons as they hide behind Lammis and Shui.

After the strings are attached to the fully inflated balloons, Lammis takes them and hands them out to the children. They delight over the floating balloons and start to run around with the strings in hand.

After seeing me float with the balloons before, I've given them to Lammis and the Band of Gluttons, who wanted them. They were jubilant, too. The kids' reactions are just what I expected.

Miss Director and Shui beam as they watch over the children. I've got the kids in the palm of my hand. I'll probably be spending all day with them, but I'll put my vending machine abilities to their fullest use and let them have fun.

Days like this aren't so bad, either.

The Orphanage and the Vending Machine

Lammis and Shui have joined the children for playtime. They're innocent and childlike in a way to begin with, so they seem to have a good affinity with kids; Lammis won them over in a matter of minutes.

Right now, the children are running away from my pressure-washer sprinkler. I've lowered the power quite a bit, so there is no danger. Just in case, though, Lammis is the one controlling it.

After getting tired out, the kids, still soaking wet, try to go into the house, but when they see Miss Director standing in front of the door with her arms crossed and a scary smile on her face, they freeze.

"And just where did you think you were going, dripping wet?"

"M-Miss Director!"

"Take off your clothes right now, put them into this basket, and go get in the bath."

"O-okay."

Withering under the director's gaze, the children begin to remove their wet clothes. Lammis and Shui strip as well— Hey, wait a minute. Maybe there's nobody watching, but you're still outdoors. This is indecent for a young woman—is what I wanted to warn them about, but it looks like I jumped the gun. They only take off their socks and shoes.

In that case, I'll provide the bath towels.

"Thanks, Boxxo. Shui, here's one for you."

"Gee, Boxxo, you're so considerate. If you were a person, you'd be super-popular!"

"He's popular already just how he is."

As if to hide my embarrassment at their praise, I form change into the coin-operated fully automatic washer-dryer combination. I'm happy to receive compliments, but when they send their raw feelings flying directly at me, I feel weird—and a little nervous.

"Oh, this is the washing one, right? I'll bring you inside."

Lammis takes me into her arms and sets me up in a corner near the front door. Then she throws the dirty clothes and underwear inside and starts the washer.

"What in the world…?"

"Boxxo is a mysterious magic item that can change into all sorts of shapes. Pretty cool, huh?"

Shui puffs out her chest and brags as though it were her personal accomplishment. Next to her, Lammis nods in an exaggerated manner. The children's eyes sparkle as they peer inside the spinning washing machine.

"Oh my. I don't quite understand it, but it certainly is amazing. Magic items these days are so helpful."

Miss Director's response reminds me of an old-fashioned mother faced with the latest electronic device. She doesn't get it, but if nothing else, she knows it's amazing. Er, not that *I'm* amazing but that Japanese technology really is impressive.

"It'll be finished washing soon, so let's all get into the bath before then. Come on, if you don't hurry, I'll catch you and slurp you all up!"

"Waaaaah!"

Shui, while sticking her tongue out and waggling it up and down, chases the children around. The children shriek and flee, but they seem like they're having fun.

If Shui were a man, this would 100 percent be a crime. Actually, even a woman would be out of the question if the children felt uncomfortable.

"If we want to wash our underwear, too, I guess we should bring Boxxo near the bathroom."

"Welcome."

You're right. I'll finish drying them in just ten minutes, so it should be done while you're in the bath.

"Oh, wait. He's heavy, so I wonder if he'll break the floor."

"In that case, if you would be so kind as to bring him around the back, you can put him behind the bathroom. There's a back door."

"Okay, then I'll go around the outside and come in that way."

Lammis hoists me onto her back, and we go around the outside wall until a door comes into sight. That must be the back door.

After she puts me down with my back against the wall, she quietly opens the door. On the other side is the changing room for the bath, packed full of half-naked and fully naked children.

Are they all going to get in at once? If they are, it must be a considerably large bathtub.

"Hey now, don't fight it. You're all in for a wash!"

Shui, naked as the day she was born, lifts up a small child and disappears into the bathroom. She has short-cut hair and favors food more than romance, but I guess she really is a girl.

"Ahh! There's no water in the bath!"

"My, my. Who was on bath duty today, I wonder?"

Miss Director, who came to the changing room to see, puts a finger to her cheek and tilts her head. As the children look around at one another, wondering who it could be, two girls raise their hands and step forward.

"W-we're sorry. We were playing with Shui, and we forgot."

As they try to make themselves look small, Miss Director gently places her hands on their heads. They give a start, then look back up and meet her gaze.

"It's not good that you forgot your chores, but thank you for being honest. Everyone makes mistakes. What's important is not to lie about them but to admit to them and learn from them."

With so many parents always scolding their kids without giving them a chance to say anything for themselves, it seems to me like it's more natural to admonish them properly—and not all that difficult, besides.

Even among my friends and relatives, some yelled at their kids so much that I felt sorry for them, and I've tried, on numerous occasions, to tell them they didn't have to get so mad. They're better than parents who don't get angry at all and leave things be, but it seemed like they overdid it at times... Still, I guess this is nothing I can get so high and mighty about when I was a single man who didn't know anything about the hardships of raising kids.

"But what will we do now? It will take time to collect water and heat it with firewood. We'll have to give up on baths for today."

If they're not taking a bath after getting so chilled from playing in the water earlier, I worry that they'll catch a cold. I wonder if there's anything I can do for them. Is there a feature of some kind?

"Oh, it looks like Boxxo's done washing. I'll take the clothes out."

It looks like even the drying is finished. As Lammis takes the clean laundry out, I skim through my features list.

Nothing to do with baths, huh? Let's see, it'll take time to heat the water, so hot water... Oh, right. I could do that.

After making sure there's no laundry left inside me, I do my third form change of the day—into a hot-spring vending machine.

As its name would suggest, this machine can automatically sell you a hot spring. It says so right here on my quadrangular prism body in Japanese: HOT-SPRING VENDING MACHINE. A hose comes out of the side, and it's set up to give hot-spring water for two minutes for a hundred yen.

I've seen this vending machine once in a blue moon at hot-spring locations, and while I've used it before, the water cools off before getting back home, so you need to reheat it.

"That's another shape I've never seen, Boxxo. How many different forms could you possibly have?"

I wonder how many there are. I've never taken the time to count, but I think just the ones I can change into number close to twenty.

"Um, this long thing is... If it's like how the other things work, something comes out of here, right? And in this situation... I got it!"

Lately, most of the figuring out of how to use machines has fallen on Hulemy, but Lammis's intuition is also quite impressive.

Hulemy tries to figure out my abilities based on the situation and my shape, but with Lammis, it's like she reads my mind to understand—as though making assumptions based on my personality.

I honestly couldn't be more grateful to Lammis for being so earnest with a mere vending machine.

She throws open the bathroom door and sticks the hose in the tub. Then she glances back at me with a wink— Is that a signal? All right, I'll release all the spring water.

The hot water rushes out, and possibly thanks to my speed stat, it fills the tub within moments.

"Wow, awesome!"

"It's a bath; it's a bath!"

"Jump in!"

"Hey! It's bath time, not playtime!"

The voices of the children and of Shui scolding them echo through the bathroom. I've finished my job of supplying the hot water, so I decide to change back into a washing machine and finish the rest of the laundry.

Lammis takes off all her clothes, too, and, from the sound of it, helps wash everyone in the bath.

"You're Mr. Boxxo, correct? Thank you very much for this. You've helped us in so many ways."

The next thing I know, Miss Director is standing right next to me.

I'm still not sure exactly how she feels about me, but she does bow her head deeply to a vending machine.

"Welcome."

"Um, that's an affirmative, right? I've been worried about Shui. She's been brooding over something recently, but seeing her like this today puts me at ease. Please continue to take good care of her."

What a benevolent person, to thank a mere vending machine and find it in herself to entrust Shui's well-being to me. Although she's acting nice, I'm really not used to situations like this—if I had a body, I'd be cringing.

Anyway, what could Shui be worried about when she has such a warm place to come home to? It probably takes a lot of funding to maintain an orphanage, so maybe she's after money. Hmm. It would be rude to pry in a situation like this.

After laundry and baths, I end up treating everyone to dinner. Figuring everyone would like foods they've never had before, I provide frozen meal sets and cup ramen. The nutritional balance bothers me, though, so for dessert I give them fruits and crepes.

The floors in the cafeteria as well as the rooms are still of dubious durability, so they decide to keep me next to the front door of the orphanage. It'd be too risky to have me on the floorboards, after all.

I thought I'd have a moment to myself to relax while the kids ate, but they said I'd be lonely by myself, so they ended up bringing the chairs and tables outside to eat in the yard.

There are a lot of empty houses around this orphanage. They probably wouldn't get that many complaints, even if they were rowdy. Immediately upon putting a forkful of food in their mouths, they shout their praise to the heavens.

"Don't eat so fast, guys. The food's not going anywhere."

Shui briskly takes care of the kids' needs. She's playing the responsible older-sister role. I know how much of a heavy eater she is, but she's putting her own meal last and prioritizing the kids.

The children's clothing is all rather plain... No, I'm being too ambiguous. They're all wearing shoddy clothing, and not one of them has much in the way of fat. Still, I can't see any overly skinny ones, either, so it seems like they're managing to eat enough food to survive.

Maybe I'll give them some underwear, T-shirts, and towels later.

I could also donate money, but would it be right to accept charity from a vending machine? At times like this, I don't know how much I should really be getting involved or how much to give. If I had the ability to talk normally, could I give aid without rubbing anyone the wrong way?

I've been thinking only of accumulating money in order to gain points, but when I look at these kids seeming so happy despite being in poverty, I start to feel like a bit of a lowlife.

"Your lights are blinking. Is something on your mind? Boxxo, you can just be Boxxo. You can afford to give everyone food for free and put smiles on their faces, right? You should be more confident in yourself."

At some point, Lammis came over to stand next to me, and she offers me words that get right to the heart of what I was feeling concerned about as she smiles sweetly.

Lammis is incredible. She takes the time to understand what a mere vending machine who can't speak is thinking, and she's so considerate. I'm truly glad she was the one who found me.

And she's right. I am me—and nothing more. I don't intend to stop saving up money for points, but from now on, I'll spare a thought for the world around me as well.

A Night in the Origin Stratum

After eating so much dinner that their stomachs seem fit to burst, the children have all settled down to sleep. We're inside a cave you can't see the sky from, so the distinction between night and morning tends to be vague, but it is apparently night right now.

Living here would probably throw off your sense of night and day.

At night, I could go into energy-saver mode, but my surroundings are just as bright, so I should be able to stay like this without problems.

Light is still coming from a window of the orphanage, the renovated former mansion; does that mean Miss Director or Lammis and Shui are still awake?

"Thanks for today, Boxxo. Everyone was super-happy and grateful and excited."

Shui sits down next to me cross-legged, and she sways, as though using her entire body to express how happy she is.

As a vending machine, I'm honored that I was able to contribute to her happiness.

Her cheeks are somewhat flushed, probably because she guzzled the cocktail I provided for the table. She thought it was just juice, so she drank quite a lot.

"I bet today wasn't cheap. I'll definitely pay you back, so just wait a little while longer."

"Too bad."

"What? You don't wanna wait?"

No, that's not it. I wanted to say she doesn't have to pay, but it sure is tough getting the subtler nuances across. Lammis and Hulemy are still the only ones I can have a smooth conversation with.

Besides, if I was going to demand money, it would be from the eatery owners. There's no need whatsoever for Shui, who won me as the victory prize, to pay.

"Too bad. Thank you."

"Um, do you mean I don't have to pay?"

"Welcome." I managed to get the point across. I'll give her a cola as thanks for understanding me.

I drop a two-liter bottle of her favorite cola drink into my compartment. For someone who eats so much, she didn't have a lot tonight for dinner, so she's probably far from satisfied. She was giving her own portion to the kids, too, so I think she's still got plenty of room left in her stomach.

"Ah, the fizzy drink! Thanks, I wasn't quite full yet!"

She opens the lid, then puts the mouth to her lips and heartily gulps down the contents. It's heavy on the carbonation, so if you drink it all at once like that, you'll—

"Whewww! Hicc— *Uuuurp.*"

Her burp echoes far and wide in the dark of night. It seems to have embarrassed even her, and she looks down, her face red.

What should I say in order to soften the mood at times like this? Okay, I got it.

"Get one free with a winner."

She blushes even harder. Must have been the wrong choice of words.

"A-anyway. Did you know that the Origin stratum is a place everyone always visits when they come into the dungeon?"

Oh, really? They were calling it the first stratum, so I'd figured it was the first floor of the dungeon.

"Too bad."

"It's set up so you have to enter this stratum first and get to the transfer circle at the end, or else you can't move to other strata. Basically, people who can't even make it past the Origin stratum don't have the right to advance to other ones."

I get it. I'd heard movement between strata via the transfer circles was free, but I guess when it comes to this one, that doesn't fly. Wait... If that's the case, does that mean innkeepers and businesspeople conquered the Origin stratum, too?

I wonder if there are hunters whose job it is to be bodyguards so other people can get through the Origin stratum.

"But if you reach the transfer circle at the end just once, you can jump to wherever you want next time."

So you don't have to get through the first stratum every time you go back to the surface? The attention to detail makes me feel like I understand the dungeon's inner workings even less now.

"A lot of the folks who couldn't make it to the transfer circle at the end of the first stratum decide to stay here in this settlement for some reason. The same goes for people who ended up having kids and couldn't advance. The kids who are born without knowing the outside world, the ones who were abandoned because they were tying people down...end up here."

So the kids at the orphanage don't know of anything outside the dungeon. In fact, they've never even moved from this stratum, either, so they've been raised without experiencing the sky, or weather, or fresh air. Hmm. That seems like it would negatively affect a child's growth.

Shouldn't they feel, at least once, the sun's light, the winds blowing around them—a world abundant with nature?

"My wish is to make everyone at the orphanage hap— Ah, I feel weirdly talkative today. Just forget I said that. I'm going to sleep! Good night!"

She swings her arms and, with an unsteady gait, disappears behind the door. Thanks to the alcohol, I was able to learn quite a lot.

All sorts of people are living their lives, with as many problems as there are Origin stratum residents. It's stating the obvious, but lately, I haven't thought about anything except my business as a vending machine and my own points.

I mean, I think that's the proper stance for a vending machine to take, but I can't quite grasp how much consideration to give. If I provide things at cheap prices or offer gratuitous service, then the eatery owners will be in a bind, and I won't get any more points. I'll have to keep the difference between business and volunteer work in mind.

◆

"Hey, is it here?"

"Yeah, bro. Word on the street is there's a rare magic item here."

I hear the voices of men who sound unmistakably like hooligans. To appear with an explanation that revealed their motive in a single sentence—they don't leave anything to the imagination, do they?

There may not be many people around, but I certainly can't call this stratum lawful, even as a kindness. We must have been too rowdy. We should have kept it down a little more.

For the first time in a while, I've encountered potential thieves. I'm kind of interested in what sort of action they'll take. Before I can see them, I put out my lights and change coloring to blend in with the dark.

"You sure? It gives you food for free?"

"Yeah. One of my guys said he saw it with his own eyes, bro."

I peel my eyes to look at the figures steadily growing closer. There are four men, big and brawny like pro wrestlers. They seem prepared to carry me—they even brought a handcart.

I'm known pretty much all over Clearflow Lake, but I'm a no-name in this stratum. Of course they'd come after me.

These men could likely carry me, too. What shall I do? If I shout and wake up Lammis and the others, they'll probably run away. But that might put the girls in danger. I'll handle things myself this time. Let's pick useful-seeming features from the ones I already have.

This one, and this—and this will be useful. I've got both Force Field and a high toughness stat. As long as nothing crazy happens, I don't think I'll be kidnapped like last time.

First, I change into a dry-ice vending machine and spread piles of dry ice on the ground near me. Next, I turn into a pressure washer and scatter water all around. When the water hits the dry ice, it creates a white mist that covers the ground in a thin layer.

After that, I turn into a jukebox and start the music.

"Hey, anyone else's feet feel awfully cold?"

"What's that sound I hear...?"

"Strange music..."

I play a song commonly heard in horror movies, and the men restlessly look around. Combined with this stratum's dimness, the atmosphere is perfect.

What should I do now? Spreading kerosene and starting a fire would obviously be going too far. If I just need to make them retreat, what would be best?

They came to kidnap—rather, steal me, so they didn't bring any light. They might be able to see in the dark, but probably not very far. In that case, I think I'll manage if I threaten them.

This time, I turn into a coin-operated, fully automatic washer-dryer combo, and with my door open, I put water into the chamber and start spinning it.

"Boss, you hear the sound of roaring wind and water?"

"There's no rivers or springs near here, is there? And there's no wind here. It's your imagination."

I provide them with some of the water in the tub by pushing it with Force Field.

"Bffwah! What, what?!"

"W-water? Where could water be coming fr—?"

"Jackpot."

They're up in hysterics, and the entire scene is pretty hilarious. Ah, I'm starting to have fun. I'll go with this one next.

I turn into an egg vending machine. My appearance changes to look like a glass-paned locker. I open all the doors and fire a volley of eggs at them with Force Field.

The eggs are packaged in nets of ten, and I fire over twenty at once, so several strike the men in spectacular fashion.

You might be mad at me for wasting food, but I'm trying to settle things peacefully here, so I'd appreciate it if you overlooked this offense.

"Ow! What's this? It's slimy!"

"B-boss, l-let's get outta here! Someone's after us!"

"Damn, they're making fools of us! We're going home for today!"

They seem to have withdrawn, so I send them off with firefly light.

Considering their behavior, they probably haven't repented yet. They'll be back. Once they know I'm not here, they could wreck the inside of the orphanage, too. Tomorrow morning when I see Lammis, I'll talk to her about how to proceed.

The amount of light in town increases, making the Origin stratum interior seem like it's brightened a bit. This must be morning here.

I've already erased the dry ice and scattered eggshells in the yard. Now the kids in the orphanage won't ever know what happened yesterday.

"Good morning, Boxxo."

"Mornin'."

The two of them appear, already energetic this morning. They're similar in a lot of respects; in this past day, they've turned into birds of a feather.

Lammis has few hunter acquaintances, so it's a relief that she made another female friend who's close to her age. The Menagerie of Fools is a source of some unease, but Shui herself is a good-natured girl, so I'm not particularly on my guard with her.

"Good morning, everyone. You two are up early."

From behind them appears Miss Director. She greets us with her usual mild expression.

"Thank you."

I've been using "Welcome" in place of "Good morning," but for her, it feels like this would be a better response, so I switched it up a bit.

Oh, that's right. If the children aren't around, then this is good timing. I have to tell them what happened yesterday.

"Huh? There's a board where the items should be. Is this the thing that showed us the map?"

That's right, Lammis. It's one of my many features—the LCD panel. If I use this to play the video I recorded last night, it should call up their attention.

As I play everything from when the thugs appeared to when they retreated, everyone watches with close interest.

"This happened last night? They're former hunters who set up in a hideout nearby."

"Looks like it. Such bad children, quitting hunting and turning to a life of crime. And to think they'd dare lay hands on a guest of the orphanage..."

Do they know them? I figured we'd bring this video as evidence to town guards or the Hunters Association and have them catch the criminals, but they failed their attempt. I stopped them before they really did anything, so all we'd be doing is reporting it.

Maybe detaining them was a little much to ask.

"Shui, I have to head out for a bit. Can I ask you to watch the children?"

"Sure, but...hang on, Miss Director..."

Huh? Shui's cheeks are drawn back, and a bead of sweat just fell from her forehead. Miss Director goes into the orphanage and comes back out a moment later, but now a large bow is in her hands. She has a quiver on her back.

"I will return shortly," she says, bowing to us before leaving.

The moment played out so naturally that no one thought to stop her. Is Miss Director going to silence them through the use of force?

Wait, that's too dangerous. One lady who looks like she's pushing sixty couldn't possibly do anything by herself. We have to go stop her.

"Ahh, it's been a long time since I saw Miss Director get seriously mad. Oh, you two seem to be worried about her, but she'll be fine. She used to be a really skilled hunter, and she trained me in the bow. In her day, she stormed through this labyrinth together with Director Bear; she's so strong that Captain Kerioyl knows she's better than him even now. Otherwise, she couldn't manage an orphanage in a place with such bad security. Plus, she's got connections to people in power, like Director Bear."

I... I see. I can't imagine that with her slender arms and general mood, but considering that Shui and the children aren't disturbed in the slightest, she must be so skilled it would be ridiculous to even worry. I should believe in her and wait.

An hour passes after that, and just as the kids are finishing their breakfast, Miss Director returns. She looks the same as when she left— Wait, looking closely, there are bloodstains on the hem of her garment, and several arrows are missing from her quiver.

"Mr. Boxxo, I've reasoned with them, and they happily acquiesced. They will never bother you again."

"Th...ank you."

My instincts, not my reasoning, told me to thank her immediately. She's still wearing that smile dripping with affection, but you can't blame me for feeling slightly intimidated by it, where I hadn't before.

A-anyway, I'm just glad this quarrel with them has been resolved. As thanks, I'll leave a week's worth of food and drink for them.

I immediately judge that she is not the type of person I want as an enemy. I wonder if Shui will become like Miss Director someday, too.

Her bow skills are amazing even now, but I don't know if the day will come when she masters *that* sort of power. With how happily she always eats her food, I can't imagine her being like that.

"Huh? It's feels like I'm being watched."

I watch Shui as she shrugs awkwardly, as if she sensed my gaze, and I accidentally say, "Too bad."

A Stomach's Limits

After continuing to observe Shui, who dominated the eating contest, there's something I've been wondering about.

Whenever she eats a large amount of food, she always wears the same blissful expression. As the one selling the food to her, I'm grateful, but I began to wonder about her stomach— Does it have a limit?

At the contest, she put away over five kilograms of fried meat and five small bottles of cola. And she ate the super-giant crepe just fine, too.

Shui is on the small side, even for a girl, and her stomach has swelled after eating before. That means it's not just that her gullet is connected to another dimension.

I've seen female eating-contest talents on TV back when I lived in Japan, too, and most ate unbelievable amounts. Maybe it's not a stretch that someone like them exists here.

But still. I've given her food many times now, and not once have I ever heard the words "I'm so full" or "I can't eat another bite" pass through her lips.

And now I've started to think that, just once, I want to hear her say personally that she's full.

"Boxxo, are you sure about this? I can really have all this for free?"

"Welcome."

Shui plops down on the other side of the table, and after Lammis arranges all the items I provided on it, Shui's eyes begin to change.

"You better not hit me with the bill afterward!"

"Welcome."

I hadn't planned to do anything like that.

We called her out to the tent Lammis and Hulemy were staying in so I could treat her to food.

The two girls seem curious about Shui's limits as well and gladly provided the space to use.

Hulemy takes a break from her work and looks closely at me. Come to think of it, she said something before. "No human can possibly eat that much and not get fat. She must have a secret. If I can find out how it works, the information will be invaluable for women everywhere," she'd said, fairly pumped up. Now she has a chart she made ahead of time, apparently planning to write down the results. Her pen is in hand—she's all set.

The issue is what to give her. I'll call it quits on the cola for a drink and use tea instead. This is purely about how much she can eat.

First, I give her five kinds of cup ramen—extra-large ones.

Normally, a person could eat two of these and be satisfied, but she'll easily get past this stage.

After pouring in hot water and waiting three minutes, she first eats the unflavored type.

"Mmm, this pasta is awesome! Whew, and it's nice and warm, too. Nothin' like eating good, hot food outside on a cold day!"

Shui really does seem like she's enjoying herself.

When it comes to heavy eaters, there are some who don't eat the food so much as devour it like animal feed. In her case, while she eats heartily, she doesn't do it in a slovenly way. Instead, it whets the appetite of anyone watching.

Her manner of eating at the contest enticed a lot of people, and items started flying off the shelves. If this were Japan, with her cute face, she'd have been hugely popular as a personality on food-related commercials.

While I was thinking about it, she finished all the cup ramen, along with the broth.

"What's next?" she asks, eyes glittering.

She's far from having stuffed herself to the brim—I'm not even sure she filled one tenth of the space.

In that case, next up is a duel against a frozen-foods manufacturer's vending machine, one the Menagerie of Fools loved.

They're used to it now—since *karaage* is part of their frozen-foods series—but it actually has quite a few items besides that.

Karaage, *yakisoba*, fried rice balls, *takoyaki*, French fries, fried rice, hot dogs, edamame, and even *taiyaki* (a fish-shaped treat filled with red bean paste) sit behind the glass.

I'll leave the sweet foods for later, I guess, and give her two other items at a time.

While bringing the food out, Lammis looks very interested at the sight of *takoyaki*, so I warm up one serving and give it to her.

"I can have some, too? Thank you, Boxxo. Hulemy, let's eat it together!"

"Sweet, I was just starting to get hungry. Thanks a lot."

They sit next to each other and dig in to their *takoyaki*. They're friendly, as always.

"These round things have sauce on them, and…something I don't know, but it's red, white, and really tasty," says Lammis. "What is this stuff?"

"Feels real interesting in your mouth, huh?"

"Oh, doesn't it? It's all chewy and stretchy. It's delicious!"

The octopus seems to be going over well. Apparently there are places outside Japan where people have an aversion to it, but people in this world eat monsters, too, so they probably wouldn't be surprised if they found out what it was.

Ah, still, even compared to the monsters here, an octopus is pretty different. If I showed them the real thing, they might refuse to eat it… Maybe I should keep quiet about them.

As they enjoy themselves, Shui finishes eating.

Now that it's come to this, I'll give her every food-related product I can provide, one by one, until one of us gives up!

Next is canned goods. First, oden, which has been a great help ever since I first arrived here. For the oddballs, I've got cans of *chikuzenni* (a dish typically eaten around the New Year in Japan, featuring braised chicken and veggies), *nikujaga* (Japanese-style beef and potatoes), *yakitori* (chicken skewers), curry rice, and ramen—well, maybe not that. She just ate a lot of cup ramen.

Incidentally, there are numerous varieties of canned noodles, and I have over ten types.

There are several flavors of canned breads, too. All right—with all this, even Shui is sure to be satisfied.

Confident, I look over and see her emptying cans, one after another… I didn't want to have to learn a new food-related feature. I'll endure it. I decided I'd use only products I can currently stock for this duel. It would be cowardly to spend points to get different items and features now.

I made light of her, thinking she couldn't possibly eat it all, but there are only two cans remaining.

Oh. Okay. I see. I… I haven't lost yet. After preparing some *taiyaki* from the frozen foods, I decide to go with crepes for everything.

I change into a crepe vending machine mainly found in Kagoshima, then get every single one of the many crepe flavors ready.

These crepes taste amazing, and they've got some hefty volume to them. Ten crepes, after eating all that, will sit real heavy in your stomach!

"Oh, sweets! I was just thinking about wanting something sweet!"

Huh? She's really happy about it.

Now I get the feeling she can finish all these off easily.

"Those look good, huh, Hulemy?"

"Yeah, they look great, huh, Lammis?"

After the two stare hard at the crepes, they turn their pleading gazes toward me, eyes watering. You don't need to give me that face. You can have some, too, of course.

Girls look happiest when they're eating sweets. All three hold a hand to their cheeks, smiling as they stuff their faces.

But now isn't the time to languish at this relaxing scene. Shui is already almost finished eating everything.

Maybe it was too early to move to the dessert course. I can't exactly go back to the heavy stuff now. What else is sweet? …Got it. I'll attack with fruit.

I pick out bags of sliced apples and bananas, but…

"Fruit is really refreshing, too!"

She gobbles it all down.

I try giving her some snack foods, too, but they immediately vanish into her stomach.

Ah. I see. I can't beat her. It seems I still need to ascend to a higher level of foodliness. With that vow in my heart, I'm about to admit defeat, when…

"Boxxo, that's enough. I'm good."

Incredibly, Shui says the words I've been longing to hear.

She rubs her belly in satisfaction—which protrudes only a little—then leans back against her chair in bliss.

Fu-ha-ha-ha-ha, I've done it! I've satisfied her stomach! I spent quite a bit doing it, but just knowing her stomach isn't a bottomless pit is enough for me—

"I've been on a diet lately. I gained a little weight at the eating contest, so I've been calling it quits when I'm around fifty percent full."

What…did she just say? Fifty percent?

That took me by surprise, but Lammis's and Hulemy's jaws drop to the floor as they stare in awe at Shui.

"That eating contest sure was fun. It would have been better if there was twice the amount of food."

I get it. I'm sorry. I humbly admit defeat.

I was naive to think I could beat Shui. I'll get my revenge after I've acquired more food-related features.

There are a few food-related vending machines I don't have yet that I've been saving for a rainy day. Once I learn them, I'll be sure to fill you up.

But for now, I admit my defeat and give her these words.

"I await your next visit."

Several months later, after rising to food-related heights that could hardly compare to my current state, I would eventually try to get my revenge. The result was—

A New Stratum

I've been continuing my business as usual in the Clearflow Lake stratum, but demand has been going down lately.

Nevertheless, I'm still turning a profit. The eateries are the bulk of my orders, and I sell them ingredients periodically. I still provide contraceptives to Shirley, too, so I'm making enough money.

If I was after more profits, I could move to another stratum and do business there, but it's nice here, so I wouldn't mind settling here permanently.

Of course, I can't move by myself, so any emigration would depend on Lammis.

"Boxxo! Captain Kerioyl says he has a request. Let's go together."

As I was lost in thought, Lammis came and spoke to me.

The captain has summoned us, has he? I heard they've been doing some investigation, so our next expedition destination may be locked in. If we're going to be fighting a stratum lord, I'll need to save up a lot of points. Both for food provisions and Force Field activations. That's my given duty, after all.

"Oh, great, you're here. Take a seat."

Lammis, Hulemy, and I, the invitees to the Menagerie of Fools's tent, sit down in front of the captain.

I haven't been in here since Shui brought me here to brag. Inside the large tent are several wooden boxes with reinforced metal frames, and some of the Fools have them open and are rummaging through them. They must keep their personal possessions inside.

"Like I said before. We've decided which stratum lord to beat next. We plan to take down the King of Souls in the Dead's Lament stratum. I'd like the three of you to participate."

Just the name of the stratum sounds disturbing. It's got to be the kind of place with all sorts of undead roaming around. And the King of Souls, is it? I imagine a skeleton mage wearing an expensive-looking robe, but I wonder what he's actually like.

"Dead's Lament, huh? If I recall, that one's filled to the brim with gross stuff like corpse fiends and skeleton fiends. Speaking of which... Lammis?"

Hulemy seems to have remembered something, and she peers at Lammis's downcast face; she hasn't said a single word. I follow her gaze... Is she trembling?

"Are we...really...g-going there?"

Why is she stammering while she's talking?

"Yeah, that's the plan. Is it inconvenient for you, Lammis?"

"Huh?! No, it's not, not really, but could we maybe...not do that?"

She's being unusually negative about this. Her voice is quiet. Could Lammis be...bad with horror-type stuff? She's clearly terrified.

"She's always hated scary stories," says Hulemy. "She's probably just scared."

"I—I am not! And I'm not a kid anymore, either, so I'll be fine!"

No matter how you look at it, Lammis is pretending to be tough. I see—so she's weak to this kind of stuff. It depends on just how horror-esque this stratum is, but it really can be too much for people who are bad at handling that kind of thing.

A long time ago, I had a friend who loved horror stuff. He showed me a lot of movies and made me go visiting haunted houses with him. My bitter experiences have allowed me to build up a bit of a resistance, so I think I'll be fine.

"Ah, you don't like scary stuff. The only enemies there are walking corpses and skeletons and maybe some ghosts—that's all. It'll be fine; I'm telling you. Hugehog fiends are way more disgusting."

"Captain, normal people are scared of these things. Not everyone can be as boldly insensitive as you."

Chided by the vice captain, Filmina, Kerioyl shrugs.

"I only know what I've heard," says Hulemy. "What sort of place is the Dead's Lament stratum?"

"Well, the sky is covered in thick clouds both day and night, with thunder and lightning flashing all the time; it's chilly; and there are gravestones everywhere that look like they're about to crumble apart."

After hearing Filmina's explanation, Lammis is now completely spooked, and she hugs me tightly. I can vaguely feel her trembling from our points of contact. She must really be scared.

At this rate, Lammis might not be able to come with us to the Dead's Lament stratum.

"Lammis, are you seriously that scared?"

"C-C-Captain! N-n-no, n-not at all. O-only little kids would be scared of gh-gh-ghosts."

"Don't force it," says Hulemy. "When you were little, you wouldn't even be able to go to the bathroom at night if you heard a scary story."

"Hulemy! You don't have to tell them about stuff that happened a long time ago!"

She's obviously embarrassed by it. At this rate, not only will she not be fighting, but she might not even be able to stick with us.

"Well, that's a problem," says the captain. "If Lammis can't go, then we have to think about who will carry Boxxo. We don't have anyone with her Might here."

"You're right," agrees Filmina. "There is nobody here who can easily carry Mr. Boxxo. However, if Boxxo is unable to come, we will be unable to go on an extended expedition due to food concerns."

"The King of Souls doesn't stay in a specific place, so it'll be a lot of work to find him. We can't be without Boxxo if we want to settle down and really search."

The captain and vice captain fold their arms and groan in thought. Even in a world where monsters roam about, ghosts and horror stories are frightening in a different way. I definitely understand not liking it, but without a means of movement, I'll turn into simple luggage.

"W-wait, everyone. It looks like you're deciding not to take me, but I'll be fine, okay? Actually, I'm great with scary things!"

She's obviously straining herself. She's different than she usually is, judging by her tone of voice.

Sometimes you can't say much without actually going there first, but… However I look at it, Lammis doesn't seem ready to handle this.

"In that case, let's visit the Dead's Lament stratum once as a test," suggests Hulemy. "Captain, there's a settlement there, too, right?"

"Yeah, there is. It's not as big as this one, but it's fine in its own right. The stratum's pretty popular among people with certain unique hobbies. I think regular people visit quite a bit, too, don't they, Vice Captain?"

"Well, most just want to see how scary it is. It goes to show there is a demand for it. Ghosts and supernatural phenomena occur on a daily basis there, after all."

It's treated as a famous horror locale, then. People who are into that sort of thing must find it irresistible. I imagine bored rich people and youngsters looking for a good time would go there.

"Let's try out Hulemy's plan," says the captain. "First, we'll spend some time in the settlement and try to get her used to the atmosphere there. If she really doesn't look like she can do it, we'll think of something else. Sound good?"

Nobody has any arguments, so we'll be moving to the Dead's Lament stratum as a test. I'm worried about Lammis—the blood has completely drained from her face—but we'll need to know how much it affects her ahead of time. It could be lifesaving.

The Dead's Lament stratum, which we traveled to by way of the transfer circle, is a place beyond my expectations.

It's even darker here than on the Origin stratum, and in the distance, I see frequent bolts of lightning and hear cries of thunder. The buildings constructed in the settlement are all moderately old and, for some reason, western styled.

Streetlights are set up at every turn, so walking isn't an inconvenience.

The residents seem to like black and dark blue; their clothing and buildings alike are in the same plain colors.

They clearly all got together and planned this. The only conclusion I can draw is that they're purposely acting this way in order to up the fear factor.

There seem to be quite a few hunters here as well, and they wear normal hunting gear, like armor and robes.

"Well, I give 'em credit for setting the tone," remarks Kerioyl. "How are you doing, Lammis?"

"Eek. I-I'm fine. Normal, I guess, really."

She's on pins and needles. She's clearly suspicious of any and every thing around her. We get it, you're scared, so calm down a little more. The residents here are giving Lammis strange looks as she trembles while carrying a vending machine on her back.

"Let's go to the inn for now, I suppose..." Captain Kerioyl gives a weary smile. He seems to have given up. To be honest, I don't think this is going to work, either.

Getting her used to this stratum is our goal, so today, our group is composed of the captain, Lammis, and Hulemy. We're just going to be spending a few days in the settlement, but I'm not even sure she'll last until tomorrow.

She jumps whenever anything makes a noise, which is shaking my view around a lot. I wonder if the carbonated drinks inside me are doing all right.

We arrive at the inn we plan on staying at for several days, but even the inn has the same spooky atmosphere.

For a building, it's not very old, and on the outside, it looks fine. But for some reason, there's ivy crawling up the walls. Even the light coming from the lantern placed in front of the entryway is just the right amount to set the tone.

It's two stories tall, but one of the windows on the second-floor corner is boarded up. I wonder why. Wait, I think I saw a woman peeking out of the gaps between the boards... It must be my eyes playing tricks on me. Yeah.

Wouldn't be strange at all for ghosts to show up in an inn like this.

If this were a horror game, it would certainly get passing marks for its outer appearance.

"A-a-a-a-are we staying here?"

She's so flustered she's turning into an actual chicken. If she's this scared, I'd love to send her back home, but she seems to want to tough it out.

"Yeah. And you know, if you can't do this, tell us at any time. We'll go back to the Clearflow Lake stratum."

"Wh-wha-wha-what're you going on about? I'm just peachy, mm-hmm, yes, sirree."

Oh boy, she's incoherent. Her accent is running rampant, too.

Hulemy sighs. "Captain, I'm with her, so we'll be fine. If things get bad, I'll bring her home right away."

"R-right. Thanks for that. I'll come up with some other way to carry around Boxxo."

I think that would be wise. But humans are adaptable creatures, so there's still a possibility, however slim, that Lammis might grow resistant to this after a little while here.

I won't get my hopes up, but I will give my all to protecting her.

Captain Kerioyl, at the front of our group, puts a hand on the entrance door and pushes. It opens with a sharp *creak*. Even that adds to the horror theme.

Past the door is a hall, but why is it darker inside than it is outside? Adding to that, the interior design is all done in black. It's easy to see what kind of mood the owner was going for.

There are also portraits hung up high on the wall, which I wouldn't think an inn needs. They look creepy, how they're all faintly smiling, but it's probably just the rest of the place having an effect on me.

It all exudes a spine-chilling atmosphere. Lammis... I understand that you're afraid, but if you put your arms around me on your back and grab me that strongly—

[1 damage. Durability decreased by 1.]

Your fingers are digging into me, I tell you! Can't you hear those awful cracking noises?

"Welcome... The Menagerie of Fools, correct? We've...been expecting you."

A woman with black hair appeared in front of us, moving smoothly without a sound. The black dress is something you'd find on a French doll, and it fits her far too well.

Her hair is so long it might stick to the floor, and you can't see much of her face, since her bangs are grown out, but her lips are so red it's like she used blood as lipstick. The corners of her mouth are turned up meaningfully into a grin.

"Heeeee..."

Oh, Lammis hit her limit. She completely froze up and then fell straight back.

Coping with Ghosts

Lammis falling technically means that I fell to the floor with her, and right now, she's unconscious and lying on top of me.

I think it's just my imagination, but I feel something damp where her bottom is touching me… It has nothing to do with this, but maybe I should give her a stylish pair of panties later.

My only consolation is that vending machines specializing in women's underwear do exist.

"Whoa, boy. I didn't think she'd have it this rough."

"You'd be surprised. This is tame compared to when she was little. I'll bring Lammis to the room. Boxxo, what will you do?"

With Lammis well and truly passed out, Captain Kerioyl takes the wooden rack's leather straps off her and puts the apparatus on his back. At this rate, I'll get in the way of the inn doing business, so I change into a cardboard vending machine for now.

"Anyone could carry you like this. Landlady, would you mind if I set Boxxo up in front of the inn?"

"Not at all… That is the one I've heard about… A magic item with a mind of its own… Fu-fu, how mysterious."

This person is the inn's proprietress? It would probably be fitting if she did something like fortune-telling as a side job.

Hulemy picks me up and places me gently outside the inn. My

regular place is steadily becoming "right next to the door." Of course, that's pretty much where every vending machine goes anyway, so I have no problem with that.

"Man, she was really scared. She's always been like that, you know. Soon as she hears a scary story, she covers her ears and starts making noises. It takes me back."

Hulemy smiles with her eyes, her expression gentle as she remembers their childhood days. She may be complaining about her now, but they're pretty good friends. Whenever I watch the two having a conversation, there are moments they look like sisters.

"Normally, she would have run away a long time ago, but it looks like she doesn't want to give in this time."

Yeah, if someone's that scared, you'd think they'd start crying and run away.

Maybe she's trying her best to endure it because if nobody is around to carry me, it will cause trouble for people. If that's the case, I'd rather she not force herself too much.

"Boxxo, you're not getting the wrong idea, are you? The reason Lammis is so gung ho about conquering her fear is… Er, actually, I shouldn't be the one to say."

"Get one free with a winner."

What was that supposed to mean? Hulemy said something deep, but now she's just giving me a sidelong glance. She doesn't bother to say any more.

Think for myself, is it? A reason she's so stubborn about overcoming this… For a girl who wants to get strong to take revenge, maybe she thinks that if she can't overcome this level of fear, there's no point.

"Well, give it some careful thought. I'm gonna go check on her."

You're not going to tell me the answer? I want to throw a question at her as she leaves, but I don't have the words for it.

It's an unsolved mystery, but I have time. I can think about it at my leisure.

"Oh, what's this? There's weird stuff lined up behind the glass. What is it?"

Whoops, it's my first customer from the Dead's Lament stratum. It's a young hunter-looking man wearing metal armor. He brings his face so close his forehead almost hits the glass to look at the products.

I guess it's time for me to do business.

"Welcome."

"Whoa! Who was that?! Was it one of you?"

"Uh, no. Sounded to me like it came from that box," points out one of his companions. And now all three stare hard at me.

"Insert coins."

"Whoa! The box seriously just talked. What does it mean, insert coins?"

The three just make a flustered racket without understanding where to put coins into. Right—normally those two words wouldn't be enough.

I always had a bulletin board placed next to me with a simple user's manual hanging on it so that first-timers could use me, too. Today, I don't have that, so I'll need to do something else.

Until now, the only thing I could do was repeat those words over and over, but I've started to get the hang of my body and features. I've scoped out various methods, and my search led me to several answers. Yes—I am an ever-evolving vending machine.

First, though it covers the items, I set up my LCD panel. Then, I play a video I recorded ahead of time.

"Whoa, there's a woman in the box. Hey, miss, do you know how to buy things from this?"

The young man talks to the woman displayed on the panel, but a prerecorded image is obviously not going to respond. Instead, the woman—Lammis—ignores them and holds out a coin.

Then she wonders aloud what she should buy as she raises her index finger and makes a pointing gesture to the viewer. After that, she stoops down, and when she stands up, her hand is holding a can of corn soup. She twists the lid to open it, then drinks it happily.

The video ends there, but I keep it playing on a loop.

"What in the world? Why is the woman doing the same thing?"

"Maybe this is an illusion? The woman there is too small to be real. And she's moving exactly the same way."

For a short while, the group discusses one thing or another, and then they appear to reach a conclusion.

"So this woman is teaching us how to use this magic item, right?"

"Welcome."

It took some time, but they managed to arrive at the correct answer. This time, they watch the video closely, and one of them, understanding how it works, buys an item.

"Nice! I bought it!"

"Oh, so that's what you do?"

"I get it."

At some point, people had formed a crowd, and now they're watching the hunters who safely bought items in admiration. They look like the ones who were interested but didn't know what I was, so they were watching me.

"You have to twist this to open it, right? Guess I'll drink it... Phew, this is great! It's cold and refreshing. It's melting into every fiber of my being!"

His reaction is the best advertisement I could hope for, and the others use the chance to buy one product after another. A lot of people are interested in both how unusual I am and the tastes they've never experienced before in this world.

I'm off to a great start. I'll save up money for a while until Lammis comes crying to me that she wants to go home.

After selling a certain amount of items, I learned that warm products sell well on this stratum. A lot of the residents wear layers, so I guess it's pretty cold here, though maybe not as cold as winter.

The temperature on Clearflow Lake was similar to early summer, and this seems closer to the opposite. My customers' breaths aren't visible, so maybe it's around fifty degrees out.

As I think about it, customer traffic drops off, and people start disappearing from the road, too. My dim surroundings are taken over by complete darkness. It seems night has arrived.

It was dark during the day, but there's a huge difference in how much light there is between night and day. There are streetlights in the settlement, but it's like the darkness is pushing their light back, letting only a tiny amount of it filter through. I couldn't say it's enough light to go by even if I was being generous.

I've experienced many nights after becoming a vending machine, but the darkness of this one feels strange. It's unnaturally dark out. There's light coming from nearby building windows, but those are the only bright places—the lights don't illuminate one bit of their surroundings.

It's just a bunch of points of light in a black world; everything else is darkness. I guess if it's this dark out, nobody would be walking around. Nothing makes the slightest sound. The sight is enough to make me start to lose my grip on whether this is reality or fiction.

The name Dead's Lament is well deserved. Maybe the dark around here is unique. If anyone is going to go hunting monsters, they should avoid the night and move during the day.

I won't be doing any business without a soul around, so I go into energy-saver mode just as some kind of faint light approaches.

Are they holding a lantern in their hand? The closer the source gets, the bigger the light becomes, but I realize there's something strange about it.

The light should be illuminating a person, but there's nothing. The light is floating on its own. It sways back and forth, maintaining about the height of a human waist as it comes nearer.

I've got a bad feeling about this. If I had feet, I'd flee into the inn this second, but unfortunately, a vending machine has no escape methods.

I'd thought that after turning into this, my mind had gotten stronger, but obviously I was wrong. I can hear an odd noise come from inside me. Telling me, a vending machine, that I'm a little scared...

Caught between my fear and my curiosity, I focus attentively on it.

It's a skull wrapped in flames. Wait, it's a flame scoll! Geez, I don't know why I was so scared. Normally it would fit right in with the horror aesthetic, but I know its weak point, and I've beaten many of them in the past. I don't need to be scared now.

Now that I know what it is, I have more room to think. My fear is gone, but the issue is that a monster has appeared inside the settlement.

If monsters normally roam the streets after dark, then we can't walk around carelessly at night.

As I'm thinking, other skulls covered with flames appear. I count eight, and those are just the ones in sight. For some reason, they don't try to go into the buildings. Instead, they just wander around, giving no hint whatsoever as to their objective.

Wait, this time a skeleton appeared along with the flame scoll. This is just a regular skeleton. And it's moving in a normal way, isn't it? Oh, and there's a half-transparent human, too. Is that what ghosts are like in this world...? This is quite the outdoor haunted house.

With so many of them brazenly moving around, they're not scary. Or rather, they're weak on the horror aspect. The ghostly, half-transparent person is walking around with regular clothes on. If they wanted to scare people, I would have liked to see a little more work put into it. Like a person with their bottom half cut off, trailing their guts behind them as they crawl and moan hatefully. Something like that. They've got a lot to learn from Japan's ghosts.

The reason I can observe them without concern is because none of the monsters is trying to get inside the buildings. Maybe the settlement residents have some countermeasure for them.

I have my Force Field up just to be safe, but the monsters don't even come close to me. They don't seem to have any interest in this vending machine.

We'll be exploring this stratum in the future, so maybe it wouldn't hurt to try out a few things. Did I have any items that could be used against the undead?

Hmm. If it's your average malevolent spirit we're talking about, then salt would do the trick, wouldn't it? Salt, eh...? You'd think I'd have it, but regular salt is one of the products that is, oddly enough, not usually found in vending machines. I have bought rock salt before, though, so let's try that out.

I drop some rock salt in a clear, cylindrical case into my compartment, then try erasing just the case and flinging the rock salt. I was aiming for a skeleton, but I miss, and it hits a ghost—and passes right through. I should have known physical attacks would never work against a ghost.

The monsters spare a cursory look at the rock salt rolling across the ground but don't give any other real reaction. As if to say it had no effect whatsoever.

What else looks like it would work... Wh-what about these? I bought these in a town in Kyoto known for its movies, at a Buddha statue vending machine: a Buddha statue and Buddhist prayer beads.

As far as I know, these are in my top-ten list of out-there products. You may not believe me, but vending machines that sell these actually exist. They're pretty small, about the size of your palm, but they're true images of the Buddha.

If I'm up against ghosts, this might have an effect. I use Force Field to fling out two statues and some prayer beads that I bought back then and watch carefully.

The monsters seem to take an interest in the mysterious objects and come closer for a look, but they don't affect them in any way. Well, maybe there's just not enough of them. I'll give them everything I've got.

"Yo, Boxxo. Man, I slept like a rock... Whoa, whoa, what's all this?! Why are there weird-looking dolls and rocks all over the ground?"

It's morning already? I was testing the effects of rock salt and Buddhist statues against the monsters yesterday. I can't believe I was going all night.

I thought it was such a good idea, too, but different worlds must have different religions!

Special Training

And so, we come to the second morning since arriving in the Dead's Lament stratum.

It's dark out, as usual, but after experiencing that night, even this level of brightness is a relief.

Captain Kerioyl seems to have moved to another stratum via the transfer circle early this morning. He said something about bringing the group that would be taking on this stratum. Also, he wanted to see if he could find anyone strong enough to carry me.

They don't have to be as powerful as Lammis, but I hope they at least have enough strength to carry me on the cart.

"Sir Boxxo… Did you have fun last night?"

As I pore over my options for the future, I discover the inn's proprietress standing right next to me… When did she get here? I didn't notice her at all. I can clearly see her, but she has zero sense of presence. If someone told me she was a ghost, I'd probably believe them.

"Around here…when night falls…monsters appear in the settlement as well… All but those confident in their skills…are not allowed outside…"

Last night's mystery has been solved. I just wish she'd told me earlier.

"The monsters here…envy the living… They are harmless to you, Sir Boxxo… I believe you came away unscathed…"

So that's why they didn't come near me and instead just peered into the buildings.

"Sir Boxxo...is closer...to them than we... No... Please excuse me..."

I'd really appreciate it if you stopped dropping cryptic lines and then leaving. Given her appearance, whenever she says something like that, I want to believe her unconditionally.

What is it she wanted to say, though? That I'm more like a ghost than a human? In that case, she's not wrong. I'm basically a possessed vending machine.

Still, I don't think I'm anywhere near as ghastly as the proprietress.

"Boxxo, sorry about yesterday."

In her place, Lammis appears, seeming in low spirits. She looks at her feet, squats, and leans back against me. Her body doesn't seem to be trembling, but she's definitely not back to her old self yet.

"Welcome."

"I've always hated scary things ever since I was a kid. I thought I got over it a little, but I didn't. At all. Uuuuggghhhhh..."

When she sighs like that it's like her soul is about to slip out her mouth. I've never seen someone faint from fear before, but it seems just as serious for the one doing the fainting.

"I said I'd be with you forever, but not at this rate, huh?"

"Too bad."

"Yeah, it is too bad..."

That didn't work. She's taking my words literally now that she's in pessimist mode. I wonder how I can cheer her up.

"Man, this isn't like you. You're the one who always acts before thinking, aren't you? If you don't like something, just overcome it. Right?"

Hulemy is here, too? Finding it difficult to see Lammis like this, she folds her arms and makes a suggestion. She looks like she's angry, but she's actually just concerned.

She's right. If she wants to do something about it, then she has to do *something*. I know it sounds like I'm oversimplifying, but that's because it really is as simple as that.

"Y-you're right! Yeah, if I'm bad with it, I just have to get used to it!"

"That's what I like to hear. In that case, I'll give you some special training to overcome your fears."

"Special training... Yeah, I can't be bad with this stuff forever. Yes, ma'am, Instructor, please train me!" Lammis thrusts a fist into the air to get pumped.

Hulemy grins at her in satisfaction. I'd like to believe I'm only imagining the slight amusement on her face.

"Then let's start by taking a stroll through the settlement."

"A... A walk, ma'am?"

Lammis gulps, her face immediately turning serious. I don't think Hulemy suggested anything unreasonable.

She takes a deep breath, turns herself around three hundred and sixty degrees, and then her hand flies up to her forehead in a salute.

"I don't think that will work, ma'am!"

"It's too early to give up. Come on—the sky is just cloudy. It's a little dark out, that's all. Nothing to be scared of. There are days like this in Clearflow Lake, aren't there?"

"Yeah, but the atmosphere is different! If Clearflow Lake is like a frog fiend, this place is like a king frog fiend!"

Her analogy is sort of understandable—then again, it sort of isn't. But, well, she's right—it's not simply dark here. The air is heavy, the humidity stifling. Water droplets stick to my body.

"Gonna give up, then? You can run back to Clearflow Lake, and Boxxo will go on the search with us. You can just sit tight."

"I don't want that!"

"Then you'll have to try harder. There's a sundries store right down the road from here, so first, I want you to go there and buy a healing herb."

"O-okay. Let's go, Boxxo," says Lammis, squatting to pick me up like she always does.

Hulemy rests a hand on her back. "Alone. Go by yourself."

"No... No way..."

"Yes way. If you can't even do that, you'll never survive outside the settlement."

"I... I'll do it. Leave it to me. I'm not some little kid. This will be easy!"

As always, the wavering in Lammis's voice is obvious. This is the biggest road in the settlement, and there are plenty of people, so even scaredy-cats should be fine.

"A-all righty. N-no use fussin' about it. This'll be a piece o' cake."

Is she going to be all right...? Now she's muttering to herself in her accent with her fist clenched.

Having resolved herself, Lammis stands up heroically, sets her eyes dead ahead, then walks bravely—for about ten steps.

At that point, she gives us a quick glance over her shoulder. Hulemy smiles and waves. Lammis returns the smile, though hers is forced, waves back, and begins walking again.

As I watch her gingerly make her way down the road, I have a thought. This must be what a parent feels like the first time they send their kid on an errand.

She makes it a few steps farther, but every time she passes someone, she's consumed by nervous trembling. Even so, she continues onward. You can do it, Lammis.

Oh, the door of the house near her just opened with a loud noise. After jumping six feet into the air, Lammis wheels around and comes running back to us at full sprint.

"Boxxoooooooooo! I can't do it!"

Ahh, now you're half crying. It took you several minutes just to get that far, but you came back in five seconds. She jumps to me and holds me, trembling fiercely.

There, there. It was scary, wasn't it? Here, you can have some warm corn soup, so calm down. Or maybe sweet juice would be better. All right, I'll drop off both of them so you can choose which you want.

Wait, if she hydrates, we'll have to worry about *that*. Not that I'm insinuating anything, but diaper vending machines do exist, so if it comes down to it, I'll...!

"Lammis... And you too, Boxxo, don't spoil her..." Hulemy puts a hand to her forehead and sighs. I'm sorry. I realize I'm spoiling her.

Still, though, if you're this scared, you should withdraw and not force yourself. If you want to grow strong as a hunter, you'll have to overcome this eventually, but for now, you're just going to have to take things slow and steady.

"Ready to go home?"

"I think I can do it if I carry Boxxo. No, I know I can! L-look, I'm in charge of carrying him, so I really think I should be the one to do it!"

Lammis is desperate. I'm happy to be wanted, but I'm pretty much in the position of being her parent.

"Fine, you can carry Boxxo, so get moving."

"Okay. I'll be fine if I'm with Boxxo. Right, Boxxo?"

I hope so. Still, I feel like the difference between going into a haunted house alone and going inside with a vending machine is like night and day... I've never seen anyone go into a haunted house with a vending machine on their back.

"Boxxo, you're there, right?! You're on my back, right?!"

"Welcome."

"R-really? You're really there?!"

"Welcome."

"Don't get off my back, okay?! Don't do that!"

"Welcome."

This reminds me of when I helped one of my relatives, a kid, who couldn't ride a bike.

I can't move by myself, so there's no way I could possibly get off her back. If she's still anxious about whether I'm still here, it means she can't feel most of the heavy weight she's got on her back right now. With the strength she has, I'd think she could smash any monster she saw at night to smithereens in one hit anyway.

"I'll do my best. I'll do my best, so let's conduct the search together. Together."

Shaking, she grits her teeth and takes one firm step after another.

I get it. I may be dense, but even I understand now. Lammis is so desperate to overcome her fear because she wants to stay with me.

In that case, I should encourage her with all my might so we can overcome her fear together. There's still quite a distance before the sundries shop. Is there any feature I have that will allow us to reach our destination with a few less frights?

Something to calm the nerves... Something relaxing... A fragrance, then? I've heard roses and grapefruits have relaxing scents. A friend of mine who was enraptured by aromatherapy was very emphatic about explaining it. Also, the smell of coffee apparently calms you down.

Should I change into a flower vending machine or a fruit vending machine, then? No, hold on. Any scent that came out if I did that would be extremely weak. I need to create a strong-enough smell that she'd be able to tell right away—maybe I'll take this one.

From my features list, I choose the aroma diffuser. This isn't the kind you use to cover up bad smells in places like bathrooms but the kind stores use when trying to attract customers.

It's the type you can easily install into a vending machine, with over a hundred scents to choose from. When the motion sensor detects a person, the scent built into the machine begins to emit the scent from a cartridge. I take the Motion Sensor feature as well to make the most of it.

The device is made for luring people in with the scent of your products, but the scent is rather strong, so it should reach Lammis, since I'm on her back.

Among the hundred scents, they have grapefruit and coffee here. Hopeful of the effects, I try emitting one.

"Ahh, I smell something good. Is it a citrus fruit?"

Oh, the trembling I felt from Lammis's back is gone. I don't know whether it actually relaxed her or merely distracted her, but she's calmed down a bit, so it doesn't matter. I'll try all sorts of other things for her sake, too. After testing a bunch of options, the two things that took her mind off her fear were the aroma diffuser's scents and the jukebox's music. I play the most effective song, a jazz piece, as I let a coffee scent drift through the air. Since I have a two-hour limit for form changes, I think sticking mainly with the aroma diffuser and only adding music in will be the most effective strategy.

I mean, the music playing seems to calm Lammis down, but we're getting freaked-out stares from the people around us. I hope she doesn't notice.

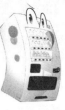

Every day, if only for a few hours, Lammis completes her grueling special training and steadily adjusts to this environment.

Her training consists of: errands in the settlement while carrying me, going to the bathroom in the inn alone at night, taking walks through the settlement with me on her back.

During the extreme regimen, there were several moments where it seemed like her spirit would break, but she overcame it all with her indomitable fortitude, and now she can freely move through the settlement as long as I'm on her back— Am I spoiling her too much?

Coincidentally, it seems there's a new spooky rumor in the settlement that tells of a girl wandering the streets with a giant metal box on her back, one who exudes a sweet scent and cheerful music. But that's beside the point.

"Hulemy, I'm all set! I don't get scared anymore."

She still gets startled enough to jump out of her boots when someone suddenly turns a corner, but she's definitely making steady improvement compared to before.

"I see, I see. I've witnessed your efforts with my own two eyes. Let's move on to the next step, shall we?"

"I don't care what it is! Bring it on!" She beats her chest, full of confidence. It looks like she's acquired quite a bit of confidence these last few days.

"There, that's the spirit. In that case, next, you'll be going for a walk through the settlement without Boxxo—"

"I can't do that, ma'am! Please spare me!"

Hulemy isn't even finished before Lammis's posture quickly bends ninety degrees in a swift bow. What splendid resolve. She didn't hesitate for a second. It looks like strolling about on her own is still too high of a hurdle.

"I think you'll be fine, since you'll always be with Boxxo during our search, but still. The question is whether you'll be okay leaving the settlement."

"I... I'll be fine. Other people will be there, too. I won't be alone."

"Well, I guess so. Come to think of it, the captain said something about bringing the search-team members today."

Oh, so we'll finally be starting this search for the King of Souls in earnest. I wonder who else will be joining us aside from the usual Menagerie of Fools members. There are a lot of undead types here, so maybe it will be a monk or a priest. A nun would be good, too.

As far as I'm aware, the healing jobs in this world go to the people with Blessings that can heal wounds. The old lady who always comes to me early in the morning has such a Blessing, I've heard.

Apparently, there is wound-healing magic, too, so personally, I'm hoping for a kind, capable woman or a warrior-priest man.

"Oh, here you are. I brought our search team today."

That voice must be Captain Kerioyl. He seems to have been looking for us while we were out and about for special training.

The two girls turn around, and I direct my view at the captain as well.

Behind the captain are the eating-contest participants: short-haired Shui the Inhaler as well as the four from the Band of Gluttons. The red-and-white twins are also here. Until this point, the members are the same as always, but there is someone else.

"I'm happy to see you again, Boxxo. And Lammis and Hulemy as well."

Jet-black armor and a cool smile. Wait, Mishuel is coming with us, too? I've no protest in terms of his combat strength, but... Will his social anxiety be all right with this many people around?

"You all know Mishuel, right? He'll be joining the Menagerie of Fools as a trial run. This is the Reclusive Black Flash we're talking about, so we'd be happy to have him. But he wants to get a clear view of our team during this expedition first. Right, Mishuel?"

"Oh, no. I simply want to know that I won't hold the rest of you back—and that I can cooperate with you all without an issue."

He looks like he's being modest, but he's serious about the second half, a fact that only I know. He seems to be replying in a normal way right now, but I bet he's sweating in nervousness in that armor.

He appears to be the only newcomer. Are there no cleric jobs in this world? That's kind of a shame.

"All right, then let's find a shop and I'll explain the expedition and give an overview of what we'll be doing," says the captain.

Prompted by him, we all enter a nearby eating house.

It's not lunchtime yet, so there are no other customers in the midsize store, and the only employee who seems to be here looks like she's at a loss at our group's sudden entrance.

"Sorry for the crowd. Can we rent the place out for a while?"

The captain flips a gold coin with his thumb and hands it to the waitress who came running up.

As soon as she sees it, her attitude does a one-eighty. She leads us to a large, round table in the back of the store, then goes to put some kind of signboard in front of the entrance door. It probably has something like RESERVED written on it.

Everyone takes their seats, placing me at the table as well, after taking out a chair.

"Get us whatever food and drinks you got. Ah, all right, the five of you need to stop giving me that greedy look. I get it. I'll order a lot."

With Shui and the Band of Gluttons staring at him through teary eyes, the captain makes a large order. With those five, our Engel's coefficient shoots through the roof. I'd think we'd be welcome customers in any restaurant.

"Now then, you can eat while you listen. Our mission is to find the King of Souls and send him to his grave. Oh, and the vice captain is on another assignment for personal reasons."

"The vice captain gets scared easily, after all," remarks Shui.

"I bet I know. She's too embarrassed to let the captain see her being scared."

"Are you serious, White? I had no idea the vice captain had such a cute side to her."

The Fools's whispering among themselves immediately elucidates the reason for the vice captain's absence. Same as Lammis, in other words. Strong-minded people tend to be weaker to ghost stories, after all.

Still, without the calm-and-collected adviser here, I'm starting to worry about this expedition. Who's going to manage us?

"Incidentally," continues the captain, "I asked for the Band of Gluttons to help because the atmosphere here won't affect them, and they're skilled at reconnaissance."

"I don't really get it, but I hear humans are scared of dark places, corpse fiends, skeleton fiends, and soul fiends," says Pell. "We don't know what that feels like."

"The corpse fiends smell bad, though," puts in Mikenne. "Like rotten meat. It makes me lose my appetite."

Pell nods at Mikenne's remark and scowls. I guess humans and beast people naturally find different things scary. Thinking about it that way, the Band of Gluttons are an appropriate choice.

Plus, they have good ears and noses. And the speed to make a quick getaway. You could call them fairly valuable assets.

"We'll be searching over a wide area, and it will be dark around us," says the captain. "Their low-light vision will be invaluable."

If I recall correctly, Tasmanian devils are nocturnal... Yeah, maybe they're ideal for this.

"And I dragged Shui, Red, and White along against their wills."

"You're a tyrant!" cries Shui. "I'm weak to scary things, too!"

"I'm not particularly good with them, either!"

"Yeah, me either!"

As his team members continue complaining incessantly, Captain

Kerioyl gives them a satisfied grin and flatly says, "You don't have the right to refuse."

The members, not to be outdone, shower him with insults, and the conversation turns into an ugly argument. We're used to them being at odds, so Lammis and the others don't bother trying to stop them. Instead, they keep quiet and eat their food.

Mishuel doesn't seem to understand the situation, but he also doesn't seem to have the courage to interrupt. He's frozen in place, a forced smile plastered on his face.

After a while, the Fools seem to exhaust their vocabularies, and breathing heavily, they sit down deep in their chairs.

"Anyway, back to the subject. Most of the enemies in the Dead's Lament stratum are corpse fiends, skeleton fiends, flame scolls, and soul fiends. Would you mind explaining what they are, Hulemy?"

"Sure, leave it to me. We fought a lot of flame scolls in the Labyrinth stratum, so I don't need to go over those. Wait, Mishuel, do you need an explanation on them?"

"No, I'm fine. Please, continue."

"All right. First up are corpse fiends. As the name implies, they're dead humans who can move around. For some, what little flesh they do have left is completely rotten, but others don't look that different from living humans. They're typically slow but powerful. Be sure not to let one grapple with or bite you."

In other words, we're dealing with zombies. In horror movies, if you get bitten, the disease always spreads. She didn't mention anything like that, though, so we shouldn't have to worry about it.

"Skeleton fiends are moving skeleton types. All their skin has fallen off, and some researchers suggest they're the end result of corpse fiends, but I subscribe to a different— Er, that's not important. They're fast-moving but not very strong. They're basically the complete opposite of corpse fiends."

Yeah, skeletons are pretty weak. I remember a certain movie where skeleton enemies got destroyed easily. Hulemy's voice isn't nervous; she talks as though they're small fries.

"Last are the soul fiends. Their bodies are transparent, and direct attacks won't work on them. They may seem like trouble, but they're weak to light. You can destroy them easily by shining any strong light on them. They won't even come near you if you have a lantern. Holy magic items and magic do the trick as well."

Is that right? They won't be coming after me, then. I should probably turn my brightness up to its maximum setting at night.

"Well, those are the monsters that appear frequently, but stronger versions of them, as well as other monsters, have been spotted here before—though not many. Don't let your guards down."

"Thanks for the explanation. With you here, we thankfully don't have to spend too much time gathering intel. We plan on leaving first thing tomorrow morning. I want everyone ready by then. At first, we'll spend half a day searching and go back to the settlement. Then we repeat the process. Won't need many supplies in that case, after all."

We'll be doing day trips at first? When I think of Lammis, that seems like a good plan. Monsters are stronger at night, and getting information on our enemies would be best on day trips.

As I think it over, I look to my side and see Lammis, her fingers digging into my body, nodding again and again like a malfunctioning machine.

Is…is she going to be okay tomorrow?

Corpse Fiend

Our big group, consisting of eleven people and one machine—my vending machine self, Lammis, Hulemy, Captain Kerioyl, Shui, the red-and-white twins, the Band of Gluttons, and Mishuel—is on the hunt. We also have the hooded buar cart with us.

We leave the settlement feeling optimistic that, with so many people, Lammis will never be scared.

"This place is as frightening as always," says the captain.

"I just remembered something I have to do, so let's go home, White."

"Yeah, Red."

"I forgot something at the inn!"

The Menagerie of Fools members all make an about-face and attempt to go back before the captain catches them. They're probably doing it half jokingly, but they're still pretty serious about it, too. It goes to show how atmospheric our surroundings are.

This barren wasteland, devoid of a single blade of grass, is littered with gravestones. Not clean-looking ones, either. I haven't seen any that have retained their original shape.

There are dead, leafless trees in all directions, but looped, thick straw ropes bundle up the ends of their branches, swaying in the wind.

...It's got the aesthetic. Old armor and weapons, perhaps the remains of hunters, also lie on the ground, racking up even more spooky points for this area.

Thunder cracks occasionally, too, and I have to give credit to the lightning's performance as well.

Anyway, while I mentally critique the place, I assess the members of the reconnaissance team. The only calm ones are Captain Kerioyl, Hulemy, and the Band of Gluttons.

"Why did they put gravestones outside the settlement?"

"Hmm, yeah, Mikenne. Why is that?"

"Mikenne, Short, you don't know, either, huh? I bet they did it on a whim."

"Maybe… But if you left grave offerings, they'd just go to waste. The monsters would eat them."

The Band of Gluttons certainly don't seem to have the same sense of fear humans do. They're not scared at all. In this sort of situation, they're extremely reliable.

"Apparently, if you die in this part of the dungeon, your very own grave appears all on its own. They're even nice enough to automatically carve your name into it."

Hulemy isn't bothered, either. She strides over to a gravestone, relaxed enough to wipe off the dust and look at the name on it with intense interest.

Mishuel's smile is firmly stuck to his face, and it's not budging. One might be impressed at how unruffled and calm he seems at a glance, but his pupils are dilated, and he's staring at a single fixed point. Is he actually petrified with fear?

Lammis, carrying me on her back, keeps her eyes on the ground, keeping any damage to her mental state to a minimum.

"You're all overreacting," says the captain. "It's a little bit chilly out here, but that's it. Real people are way scarier than some dumb corpses or monsters. Don't let the atmosphere get the better of you."

The Fools clench their jaws and firm their resolve, though their faces are still pale with terror.

Mishuel snaps out of it and clears his throat, once again donning his cool, composed smile.

They were unnerved for a bit, but they've gone right back to normal, so it probably won't be an issue. Lammis is still staring at the ground, so we can't expect anything from her in combat, but if she's just in charge of carrying stuff, she'll be fine. I hope.

Captain Kerioyl sighs. "Well anyway, let's not worry so much about the destination today." He takes off his hat, an unusual gesture, and scratches his head. He's probably annoyed by the many difficulties he sees us having in the future, and I can't say I blame him.

If the Band of Gluttons turn out to be the most reliable in this situation, I'd want to sigh about it, too.

We wander about, mostly at random at the captain's instructions. The enemy-encounter rate is fairly high. Just strolling around for thirty minutes, we run into over ten monsters to fight.

And just as I'm reflecting on it, more appear.

The ground swells, and a white-boned arm comes out of it, its flesh appearing to be in the middle of some very important rotting.

Other arms and skulls, already dry bones, push their way out of the earth as well, following the rules and coming out close to gravestones.

It looks like zombies—or rather, corpse fiends and skeleton fiends—but four are destroyed with ranged attacks before Lammis can take a breath, and before the other four bring themselves all the way up out of the ground, the Band of Gluttons close in and crush them with fang and claw. It would seem our great army is invincible.

I understand it's an efficient way to defeat them, but I feel a little bad for them.

Despite their earlier fear, the Menagerie of Fools move crisply and accurately during battle. Mishuel does, too—when a battle starts, he activates his hot-guy mode without issue.

Which just leaves Lammis. When enemies appear, she holds her breath and freezes, but she doesn't cry out or try to run. Personally, I think she's come quite a long way.

Enemies continue to go down pretty easily after that, but Lammis seems to be concentrating fully on carrying me and never takes part in a battle.

*   *   *

The party returns to the settlement before night falls and quickly withdraws into the inn.

As always, I sit outside, staring idly at a night sky with no visible stars in it.

After learning the monsters here wouldn't do me any harm, I've been treating myself to bouts of monster watching at night during my spare time. Moodwise, it feels like sitting in an expensive chair, wineglass in hand, watching a horror film.

Never learning their lessons, the monsters wander through the settlement again tonight, peering into windows with light coming from them. After observing for a few days, I realize that despite their unchanging expressions, it's started to look to me like they're staring into the rooms with envy for some reason.

Rumor has it that these monsters, unlike normal ones, are based on people who have died. Maybe I can't discount the idea as nonsense.

"Ahhh, ah, ah, ahhhhh."

While I'm ruminating, I hear a voice from very close by, so I immediately look ahead.

It must have closed the distance quickly before I knew it. Now I'm face-to-rotting-face with an honest-to-goodness zombie, flesh peeling and one eyeball about to fall out.

Ah, yeah, okay, it being this close is a little rough. It's illuminated by the light emitted from my body, too, and its crisp shadow adds to its impact.

Instinctively, I try to cry out, but I end up saying, "Insert coins." I hate this body for having nothing but canned phrases to say at times like this.

Hearing the voice come from my body saying something that doesn't fit the situation makes my shock and fear subside. To think saying it would calm me down...

Since I'm calmed down again, I'll take a good look at it. The thing in front of me has got to be a corpse fiend. It's short in stature, so it's probably a child.

Maybe because I'm an unusual sight, it says "Ah, ah" and looks at me with its remaining eye. If it's true that they're based on people, does that mean this corpse fiend lost its life at a young age and turned into a monster?

Just the thought makes the concept of corpse fiends a whole lot less terrifying. It doesn't want to cause me any harm. If it's just staring at me with childlike curiosity, then there's no reason to be mean to it.

Okay, stop that. Get your dirty hands off me. Fingerprints are the least of my worries when rotten flesh is sticking to me. Oh, fine, then I'll give you this.

I don't know whether it can drink, but I drop orange juice, a favorite of the twin-tailed rich girl, into my compartment.

It reacts to the clanking of the can falling, but can it not understand what it is? In that case, I'll try flinging the orange juice out with Force Field.

It rolls past the young corpse fiend. After reacting to it and turning around, it heads for the juice, its body swaying back and forth with an uneasy stride.

They must be the type that gets overly distracted at noise, which is common in zombie films.

It grabs the can of orange juice with both hands. As I watch over it and wonder what it will do about the lid, it bites into the can. Its teeth easily pierce the aluminum, and orange liquid comes out from between them, dripping onto the child corpse fiend's body.

It continues to chew, aluminum can and all, until it seems satisfied and goes away, disappearing into the darkness. That was an unexpected encounter, but I'll probably never meet it again. It's been an odd night, but strangely, I didn't mind it.

Our second day of searching comes to an end, and I sit outside watching the twilight.

Like yesterday, Lammis didn't take part in any battles, but she managed to keep her eyes looking forward and properly watching the battle. Yeah, that's the way.

"Ahh, ahhhhh."

The corpse fiends and soul fiends are springing up again. It's like they only come to every day for a wandering nighttime walk.

As I watch the monsters go by, one walks straight over to me right from the beginning. Could it be the same young corpse fiend as yesterday?

Its rotting face and pulled-out hairstyle look the same, but there's no proof. It would be easier to identify if there was some sort of defining feature, but it's hard to tell the rotted faces apart. I guess I'll know if it's the same corpse fiend if I give it orange juice.

Like yesterday, I fling some orange juice outside my Force Field. It picks it up, chews up the whole thing again, and leaves seeming satisfied. Wait, did it get attached to me? No, that can't be right.

Night number three...and the young corpse fiend is here again.

Did it acquire a taste for it, like many kids do? Maybe in that rotting body, even after turning into a monster, traces of its childlike habits and instincts remain.

Maybe this sort of thing is pointless, but I give the kid orange juice again. Even I'm not sure what I want to do, but interacting with this kid is on its way to being something I look forward to in the middle of the night.

The fourth, fifth, and sixth days pass. The search is going smoothly, and today, for the first time, we'll be spending the night outside the settlement. Of course, we're only a ten-minute walk away, so if something happens, retreating won't be an issue.

I feel sorry for the young corpse fiend—it's come back every night since I first encountered it. I won't be able to give it orange juice today. Well, it'll have to bear with it until we get back tomorrow.

"Boxxo, let me sleep next to you tonight."

Everyone has formed a ring around the fire, but I've been placed a little farther away to avoid the open flame. As I sit there, Lammis, wrapped in a blanket, snuggles up against me.

She did a good job making it through the scariness all day long. I'll gladly sleep right here next to you. You'll be in my care, so don't worry.

"Welcome."

"Thanks, Boxxo."

The extreme tension must have worn away the last of her stamina, and sleep takes her in a matter of moments. Good job today, Lammis. Let's work hard again tomorrow—together.

I'll have to remain alert of our surroundings in order to protect the soundly sleeping Lammis from danger. The night watch today includes Mikenne and Short from the Band of Gluttons, a levelheaded combination. The red-and-white twins round out the lineup.

They've got enemy detection and response down pat, so I could rest easy knowing they have things under control, but there's no telling what could happen in this world. It wouldn't hurt to have one extra person on the lookout.

Nobody seemed to have the heart to cook out in a place like this, so everyone bought their meals from me. It was a pretty good haul.

Midnight approaches, and as even the lookouts start to lose focus a bit, I hear a soft noise.

"Ah…ahhh…"

A corpse fiend? There's only one, but its voice is steadily getting louder. It seems to be heading this way.

"Red, should we wake the others?"

"If it's only one, we should be fine, White."

The two from the Gluttons remain alert; it seems the red-and-white twins will deal with the noise drifting over from my direction.

They come up next to me, and I increase my light so we can see the enemy better.

What appears from the darkness is a small corpse fiend… Wait, it's that one!

"A child? I feel sorry for it, but it's time to rest in peace!"

"TOO BAD!" I shout at maximum volume in order to stop Red, who leaped out, but he thrusts his spear into the young corpse fiend's stomach without turning back.

"What, Boxxo? Why did you suddenly shout like that?"

Red looks at me, confused, not knowing what I meant, but that doesn't matter. That child corpse fiend, was it the one—the one who always came to me at night?

"What? Something's stuck to my spear. Wait, this is the container for one of Boxxo's drinks, isn't it? Where did it get this?"

Without a doubt, the thing his spear has pierced is the fragment of an orange juice can.

I know it wouldn't make sense to get mad at Red. For him, the child corpse fiend was just another monster. He should be praised for dealing with it so swiftly, not criticized.

Of course I know that…but when I see it fall on its face, hand stretched toward me, I feel my wiring almost short-circuit.

This kid probably found me and came to get juice like it always did. But that's just my assumption—it could have actually come here to attack people.

That's right. Anyway, it's past the time that kid usually comes. This one is probably a normal monster, and its instincts are to attack people—

"Red, is it holding something in its hand?"

I look over after White's remark and see that the young corpse fiend's hand, outstretched toward me, is gripping a coin.

"Could it have come to buy something? No, that's impossible. Right…?"

"I don't know if it was this one, but there's been one watching us from a distance for a while now. It wasn't bothering us, so we ignored it."

Mikenne interrupted their conversation. He's nocturnal and has night vision, so there's no reason not to believe him.

In other words, this kid mimicked the process of buying something with a coin and came to try to put the coin into me…

You idiot… Kids shouldn't have to worry about that. Besides, that's a copper coin you're holding. It's not enough…

Even after Red and White lose interest, I can't look away from the child.

I change into a coin-operated vacuum. After some struggle, I suck up its copper coin, then revert to my usual vending machine form and add orange juice to my stock.

You liked this, right? You want the usual, don't you?

I change the orange juice so that its price is one copper coin, then drop it and roll it over to the corpse fiend.

Then, I offer my first and last words of gratitude to the child.

"Thank you."

Future Direction

One week into our search, even Lammis seems to have grown fairly accustomed to things, and now she can fight monsters other than corpse fiends. Given their visual appearance, I don't blame her for hesitating to use her fist to crush them.

I have an attachment to corpse fiends after that incident, so I appreciate not having to watch her smash them to pieces up close.

"Captain, you did think of a plan for when we do eventually run into the King of Souls, right?" asks Hulemy, poking her head out of the cart. Since there's no place for her in battle, she's been rustling around in the cart all the time lately.

"Hmm? Oh, right, well. This might be rude of me to ask someone as smart as you, but do you know what kind of monster the King of Souls is?"

The captain, who's been walking leisurely next to the buar cart, turns his head and answers her question with one of his own.

"He's that one, right? Basically a mega-size skeleton wearing a pricey-looking robe, right? Real snobbish kind of getup? I've heard people say he's the shade of a formerly great magician."

"Well, they're not wrong. He can use lots of elemental magic, and he apparently has a ton of mana, so he can fire multiple spells in succession.

This might not be much of a consolation, but his body is pretty frail, apparently."

That makes him a completely magic-specialized type. We could probably win by hitting him with something huge, but it'll come down to how we get around his magic and get in close.

If we need brute force to fell this opponent, Lammis or Mishuel fits the bill.

"So what do we do against the magic? We don't have any shields or walls in this group. And even if we did, magic isn't physical, so they wouldn't help."

The "shields" and "walls" Hulemy mentioned aren't meant literally—they're apparently roles hunters can have. In other words, teammates specialized in defending allies by drawing in an opponent's attacks and withstanding them.

"Well, we do have someone suitable in the Fools, but there's no point quibbling over someone who's not here. But we have someone here who we can rely on to defend all kinds of attacks, don't we?"

Winking, making a mischievous expression, and casting a glance over in my direction is a certain stubbly old man.

Oh, I see how it is. I just realized why you were so persistent in taking me along on the search.

"Wait, do you mean Boxxo?"

"That's right, Lammis. His Force Field is an almighty shield that can even protect against magic. You can push right in to take the King of Souls down—or just draw his attention for us. Either way works."

"That's rather... Well, maybe it's not so dangerous. Boxxo has already proven he can withstand a stratum lord's attack. I hear he defended against the magic the guys after Mishuel had used, too... Maybe it's possible..."

Hulemy seems to be thinking things over, tapping her forehead with a finger in a steady rhythm.

I have plenty of points to spare, so I'm confident I can protect against his attacks. As for the concern of a high-power strike blowing me away, since Lammis will be carrying me, she can deal with it by keeping her footing.

Wait, this is a surprisingly well-devised plan, isn't it?

"Boxxo, what do you say? If you don't think you can, we'll rethink it. Can you do it?"

In terms of whether it's possible or impossible, it's possible. It would expose Lammis to danger, but that just means I have to protect her. She chose the dangerous life of a hunter, so she'll never progress by avoiding things just because they're dangerous.

"Welcome."

"Hah, should have expected that, Boxxo. What a man."

"If Boxxo is okay with it, then I'll do it."

Lammis has absolute faith in me. A man has to respond to those expectations. I may have become a vending machine, but I must always have spirit.

"Since the King of Souls is called a king, he'll probably appear with several other monsters in tow. You can leave the small fries to us."

I don't even have any room to doubt the Menagerie of Fools's abilities. The same goes for Mishuel. I think the Band of Gluttons would have difficulty fighting corpse fiends, but they're quick and light on their feet, so they won't get captured. And they're stronger than the skeletons, so no problem there.

The more I hear, the more I feel like we can do this.

"But this is all just theorizing. The fundamental rule is to adapt to any situation. If things get bad, we run away as fast as our legs will carry us. Make sure you're listening for my instructions."

I don't hate his style of saying it's okay to run away instead of pressing the attack even if people die. No matter what you might say, the Menagerie of Fools care deeply about their comrades' lives. That's probably why his members like him, despite their complaining.

"Can I ask one more question?"

"You can ask whatever you want, Hulemy."

"I don't think it's a bad plan, but how did people before now defeat the King of Souls?"

Oh, right. He formulated this plan around my Force Field, but I'm interested in how other hunter groups beat him before now.

Still, after putting this strategy together, the other members haven't talked at all, as though they were in the dark about it. Normally, the vice captain would be here, but Hulemy's position is unchallenged right now.

"Other people? As far as I know... They bulldozed through him with numbers, regardless of the sacrifices. I also heard some challenged him with perfect countermeasures against magic. Our plan is closer to the latter."

The former type made the worst choice. I can't say it's a mistake to rely on numbers if you don't know how strong something is, but how many fell in sacrifice to that?

"I've got all the detailed data on his traits and methods of attack, so give that a look-over. Lammis, you give Boxxo the rundown, too."

"Okay, I will. Boxxo, let's have a study session later."

"Welcome."

I can't read letters, so I'm relying on you, Lammis. I'd like to finally learn how to read this world's language soon, but I can't even think of a way to get someone to teach me.

Literacy doesn't seem low in this world, and among the people living in Clearflow Lake, at least, I've never seen someone having problems because they can't read letters. The letters look kind of like a broken version of the English alphabet, but without real learning resources or someone to teach me, it'll be too hard to learn it on my own.

"There you have it. I want all of you to know it like the back of your hand."

"Yes, sir!"

The Fools and the Band of Gluttons raise their hands. A soul-soothing sight, as always.

I'll commit everything to memory later, too. If I can get information on this enemy, I might be able to think of countermeasures based on my features.

"That about wraps it up. Get all that?"

"Yes, Teacher!"

Hulemy, wearing glasses for some reason and holding a pointing stick, finishes her detailed explanation to everyone as they hold their copies of the document. Her tone is rough, but she's actually a very nurturing person, so everyone likes her.

I'll go over the information in my mind.

When the King of Souls appears, several monsters also materialize around him. The number is random, and apparently, close to fifty once sprang up. I'll have to remember that we're withdrawing right away if there are any more than thirty.

The King of Souls uses mainly magic attacks, freely able to cast the four major elements—fire, water, wind, and earth—and is also skilled in dark magic. He seems weak to light magic and doesn't like brightly lit places, either. It might be possible to shine my light at full brightness to scare him or something.

He's weak to physical attacks but strong against magic. Magic barely affects him, so we'll be taking a direct approach.

Also, Lammis and I will be ignoring the small fries and going after the King of Souls. Ideally, I'll repel his magic with Force Field as we get close, then we'll destroy him right off the bat. If we can't, though, we'll just have to draw his attacks. It seems simple when put that way, but unlike me, Lammis is an actual person. I've been entrusted with her protection, so I'll defend her with all my might.

In other news, everyone gets some healing medicine as well. Apparently, sloshing it over smaller wounds is enough to heal them. There's one thing this world has in common with fantasy games.

Now, if we find the King of Souls and it comes down to a fight, it'll be my third time fighting a stratum lord, won't it? What do you think of a vending machine getting such good results as a hunter?

It might be the ideal development for stories where people get transported to other worlds, but a vending machine is… No, I shouldn't think that way. That I'm living a fulfilling life in another world *despite* the fact that I'm a vending machine is something I should consider happiness.

And I'm not just luggage, either—I'm helping out. That's something I can be proud of, right?

"We got the important role, but let's do our best!"

"Welcome."

Of course, Lammis. I ended up snatching the kill on the last stratum lord, so let's treat ourselves to a group stratum lord beatdown. In my opinion, Lammis's abilities deserve way more praise.

After all, my personal goal is to become a famous duo with her.

Now that she's gotten accustomed to this stratum, and her fear has waned, I can expect Lammis to perform well, too. We can't let arrogance get the better of us, but the more active we are, the less danger our comrades taking part in the battle will face. That's something both Lammis and I want.

"Lammis, don't get too worked up," says Hulemy. "If worse comes to worst, and one of us dies during the fight, it's nobody's fault. Everyone's here because they agreed to be here. Don't forget that."

She puts a hand on Lammis's head. She has zero combat ability, but she's absolutely indispensable for providing both information and moral support.

The other members all give deep nods as well. Nobody wants to die here, nor do they plan to. I guess they have to be prepared, though.

I don't want anyone to die, either. Even bad people have rights; killing is wrong no matter the reason— Yeah, I don't believe that for a second. It's not like it affects me when people I don't know from places I've never been to die.

But I still don't want anyone who has used me even once to die. I know that's an unreasonable wish when it comes to those in the hunting profession, who are always face-to-face with death.

Even so, I hope from the bottom of my heart that we can return to the settlement with nobody missing so they can buy things from me again.

"Well anyway, all that only happens when we find the King of Souls. Let's cheer ourselves up with some of that fizzy drink."

"I had some during the eating contest, too, and I'm hooked," says Hulemy.

With that, I start selling cola until everyone has one.

"All right, why don't we all have a toast?"

"Agreed! Let's open the lids, and... Cheers!"

"Cheers!"

Everyone forms a circle and clinks their plastic cola bottles together, then drinks, smiles on their faces.

I feel like I'm watching a certain cola company's commercial. After this search is over, it wouldn't be so bad to get everyone together again for another toast over cola.

Decisive Battle

"Captain, I got a report from Red saying he spotted a monster just ahead that matches the King of Souls's description."

Thanks to the Blessing that allows the red-and-white twins to communicate with each other over long distances, we were able to receive a report from Red and two members of the Band of Gluttons who had gone out for reconnaissance.

"Found him, did he? Have them keep a set distance and continue watching. Let's hurry there."

Here we go. I've done several simulations in my mind, so I think we'll pull through, but if the situation calls for it, I'll devote myself to defense.

The question is what Hulemy, the noncombatant, will do, but she's heading to the scene along with the buar cart. They've taken the hood off the cart, and Shui is riding in it as well, set up to provide ranged attacks.

She has Suco and Pell from the Band of Gluttons as guards as well, so she decided she would be fine. Either way, we can't leave her behind, nor can we afford to go back to the settlement.

"We should get there in about ten minutes," says Captain Kerioyl from the driver's seat, his hands gripping the reins. "Prepare yourselves."

Everyone nods.

The Menagerie of Fools and Hulemy are all on the buar cart, which is proceeding at a decent clip, with the Band of Gluttons and Lammis running alongside it.

I know I should be used to it already, but it still surprises me how strong her legs are to easily push out this much speed with me on her back. Once she can freely control her power without having anything else, she'll probably gain so much strength nobody could beat her. But for now, she still seems to have trouble controlling it. She'll just have to practice again and again to get her body used to it.

"There they are."

Behind a boulder in front of us are Red and the Band of Gluttons's Mikenne and Short. They wave to us. We slow down as we approach, and for now, everyone hides behind the boulder.

"What's it looking like?"

"The King of Souls is up ahead, along with a group of monsters we think are his subordinates. Five corpse fiends, five soul fiends, eight skeleton fiends, and four flame scolls."

The simple question garners an appropriate response. His cronies number twenty-two. It's within the allowable range we decided on beforehand, but it's still a little much.

"We can take them, but... We'll want to take out as many as we can in our opening move."

"And we don't have the vice captain," comments Shui. "Though a bow would pick off a few before they got close."

How can we take them all out at once? We don't have magic, so our ranged attacks are limited to a bow and the captain's throwing knives. With the Band of Gluttons's hands, they can't handle throwing weapons, and Lammis's accuracy is too low.

I could put out the flame scolls' fires by using the pressure washer to shoot water, but it won't do anything against the other monsters. Red explained that the monsters are positioned in a ring around the King of Souls, so maybe we should be using those flames instead. In that case, why not change into a kerosene meter, scatter the kerosene, and turn the entire area into a sea of fire?

Huh, that might actually be a good plan. To be safe, maybe I should use gasoline or diesel, since they have lower flash points. There's a gas pump right there in my features list, after all.

"If we can eradicate the small ones, it would be easy... Oh, Boxxo, you think of something?"

Captain Kerioyl's eyes widen when he sees me change shape. I don't mind if someone has high expectations of me, but the issue is whether they'll quickly understand how to use this.

At first glance, it's a square body that looks like a normal vending machine, but it has red, yellow, and green nozzles stuck in it. An adult Japanese person would understand, but the red nozzle gives regular gasoline, the yellow gives high octane, and the green gives diesel.

Lammis, apparently having her own ideas, sets my form-changed body onto the ground and stares intently at me. Here's where the problem comes in. How can I get them to understand?

"This looks like the apparatus that shot water," says Hulemy. "Can I pull this out?"

"Welcome."

At a glance, Hulemy realizes what it is and pulls out the diesel nozzle. She looks at it in her hand. I'm glad she understood that much, but...

"Yeah, this looks like the same tool that shot water. Something will come out of the tip when I pull this, right?"

"Welcome." Thankfully, she already knows all about the pressure washer.

"I'll pull it. Is that all right?"

Of course. That's exactly what I want. "Welcome."

Hulemy turns the tip away from everyone else and pulls the lever. Clear liquid begins to gush out of the nozzle. There's normally a safety feature on these so the gas won't come out unless it's in a tank, but I had that disabled.

"Ack! That smells awful!"

The Band of Gluttons hold their noses and scowl.

Hulemy releases the lever, and after putting the nozzle back where it was, she squats and begins investigating the diesel that leaked onto the ground.

"Boxxo, can I touch this? It's not poison or anything, right?"

"Welcome." A little touch won't cause a problem. The most it'll do is make her hand smell.

"Man, this really stinks. It feels slimy, like oil. I'll try soaking some paper in it."

Hulemy holds the paper damp with diesel away from her, then takes out a cylindrical object the size of her palm from her pocket—it's a fire-igniting magic item.

At one time, I'd considered selling hundred-yen lighters to see if they would take off in this world, but then I learned that magic items that accomplished the same thing were common, so I gave up.

A flame lights on the magic item's tip, and she brings it close to the paper.

"Whoa! I thought it was oily, but this stuff really burns!"

Hulemy quickly lets go and observes as the paper continues to burn on the ground. The grin she's making, illuminated from underneath by the flaming paper, is somewhat frightening.

"I get it. You want us to splash them with this super-flammable oil, don't you?"

"Welcome." That's correct, Hulemy.

"In that case, I should run at the enemies and spray the oil at them, right?" asks Lammis.

"Yes, but…," says Hulemy. "No, wait. There's a better way to use this oil. Boxxo, can I use a container with water in it?"

Having thought of something, Hulemy's lips curl into a smile. I see it and understand. Of course—use them to your heart's content.

"Welcome."

We finish our work before the King of Souls moves and then get ready for battle.

"Let's do things the way we planned. Don't forget your roles… Let's go!"

Everyone jumps out from behind the boulder. Lammis and I lag slightly behind our comrades as we all plunge toward the King of Souls from the front.

There's still some distance, but he seems to have noticed our movement. For now, he orders his underlings to attack us.

When the monsters leave the King and head for us in a single mass, everyone throws the plastic bottles in their hands. Lammis instead pulls out the diesel nozzle, though, and points it at the enemies.

When the plastic bottles reach the peak of their parabolic arc, I erase just the bottles, letting their contents—the diesel—pour all over the monsters' heads.

The flame scolls' flames ignite the diesel, turning the surroundings into a sea of fire. With the diesel shooting from the nozzle spraying around, too, the flames intensify.

Their comrades split up to the left and right, trying to avoid the patch of ground suddenly on fire. We, however, calmly plunge right into the flames.

With my Force Field not letting any fire, heat, or carbon dioxide inside, we dash through the fires in one burst.

I can't see anything through the flames, but the same goes for our enemies. Because we stagger our exits, the King of Souls should be seeing our comrades leaping into view among us.

With our enemy's attention elsewhere, we dash through the flames and jump out.

Bingo! About thirty feet until we're right in front of the enemy. There stands a skeleton in a jet-black robe with gold embroidery everywhere.

It seemed about to cast a spell, but when it sees us, it switches targets. The skeleton puts one arm on top of the other and points a newly created staff at us.

Here comes a spell! My Force Field is up and ready. I'll block any magic, for sure, no matter what it is.

From base to tip, its staff was made entirely of skeletal arms with fists closed tightly around one another, but suddenly, the hands all burst open with a flash of light.

Lightning?! Electric-type attacks have the worst compatibility with a vending machine. With Force Field, I don't let a single bit of static in, repelling all of it. In that moment, I thought I saw a red light glimmer in the King of Souls's lifeless eye sockets. Is he confused?

"You blocked my magic?! That pale-blue light, is it…Force Field?! What impudence!"

Whoa, the skeleton talked. It's a surprisingly nice voice, very regal. I guess it would be stupid to complain about how he can talk without any vocal chords. After all, I'm a vending machine, but I have a will.

If he recognized my Force Field at a glance, then maybe he really was a superb magician during his lifetime. In that case, we have to crush him with a swift attack before he can put his true abilities on display.

While his attention is on us, Shui and Captain Kerioyl lob arrows and throwing knives at the King of Souls.

"How futile."

The King of Souls swings his staff a little, and from both his sides appears a wall of bones, made up of tightly packed skeletons. He swings the staff a second time, which causes the skeleton wall to collapse, but the skeletons themselves descend to the ground and rush for our comrades to attack.

One layer of that wall has thirty skeletons. If they're up against a total of nearly sixty, we probably can't hope for any support.

"You there, the girl. That box on your back... There's something about it, isn't there?"

"I don't really know!" replies Lammis offhandedly to the question, charging in.

From here on out, it'll be one-on-one plus one. This is the first time we've gone up against a boss-class enemy by ourselves. Let's give it everything we've got!

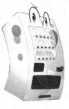

"Stones of ice, pierce!"

The King of Souls mutters spell-like words, and then pieces of ice with sharpened tips fill our view. I count up to ten of them before giving up.

"We're going in!"

"Welcome."

No worries—I'll block all those little things.

The ice impacts against the Force Field's blue wall, but none has gotten through yet.

[Points decreased by 1. Points decreased by 1. Points decreased by 1—]

I'm losing points by the second, thanks to this icy onslaught. The endless notifications wash over my mind like a waterfall.

But I still have a lot of points left, so this level of point draining isn't a problem at all. I'm still kicking.

"Hmph. Such a troublesome Blessing. Does it belong to the girl there—? No, this is something coming from the soul residing in the magic item behind you. Fire, in that case... No, you ran through it. Then what about raging, howling winds?"

First a rain of ice, now a windstorm? A few more steps, and we would have reached him, too.

The wind crashes down on us from the front, digging a hole in the ground outside the Force Field and blowing gravestones back behind us.

I mean, I'm blocking the wind, but since the Force Field is increasing our surface area, we're taking the brunt of its effects now.

"Fu-ha-ha-ha-ha. It may be an impenetrable barrier, but there are plenty of ways around it. I'll blow you and that Force Field away— Hmm?"

The King of Souls, in the middle of a victory celebration, opens his mouth and stares at us.

Within the gales strong enough to tear the very ground asunder, Lammis continues forward, little by little. The wind pressure is incredible, but Lammis presses on, digging her feet in and leaning forward.

"What is the meaning of this? Why have you not been blown away? Are you using magic to interfere with my gales?"

No, it's simple brute force. She's physically resisting them.

"I won't lose to some wind, some hail— Attack, smash, smash!" As Lammis muscles her way forward, she mutters some disturbing things.

"If ice, wind, and fire have little effect…how about this? Lands beneath, cry out in lament!"

Does he really need to say that line for his incantation? I think it's cool, but it makes me cringe every time I hear it. Yeah, I feel like that extreme escapism that afflicts every boy in their second year of middle school is starting to relapse.

But now's not the time to be thinking about stupid stuff. As I feel shaking from underfoot, a fissure begins to run through the ground. Then, with a thundering roar, the land splits in two, and an abyss opens its mouth wide.

"W-wait a minute!"

Lammis begins to fall upside down. I can't leave her to her fate. I form change into a cardboard vending machine. That makes me lose several hundred kilos, which should lighten her load.

"Th-this is nothing!"

Lammis kicks off the side of the depths and leaps diagonally upward, then kicks off the opposite side. Seeing her repeat the process, kicking off the wall to advance up, is like a ninja action video game.

"You were a somewhat formidable opponent. Close, O jaws."

The fissured earth begins to close steadily, but before it shuts all the way, Lammis kicks one more time and leaps high into the air.

"What?!"

He watches Lammis in shock as she flies up out of the abyss. We're about thirty feet over his head now. She gave that one everything she had. With the King of Souls right below us, we're in a perfect position.

"Um, in any case, kiiiick!"

After reaching the peak of her jump, she begins a rapid descent, falling with a kick. Still, Lammis has only so much power with her body weight. No matter how strong her Might is, she has to plant herself in place or else her power goes down.

Adding to her attack power now means increasing her weight. It's simple. It means I—

"You think that miserable kick will work?! I'll shoot you down. Assemble, assemble, assemble, from the abyss you come, O evil from the den of iniquity—"

Not going to happen. I change into the giant vending machine that's over ten feet tall, which I've turned into before. It adds only a little bit to our speed of descent, but it throws off the King of Souls's timing. Plus, he's startled by how I changed shape in midair. He stops his incantation, and we connect with his face.

"Urgh!"

Her soles dig in, and even I feel something breaking on the other end.

"Oh, whoa! Hup!"

Lammis kicks off the King of Souls's face and drops to the ground. Her body shudders when she lands, but she manages to pull herself back up before clenching a fist and burying it in the core of our enemy's body.

In contrast with her cute cry, an explosion rather than a mere punching noise rattles the air. The King of Souls lurches forward brilliantly and gets blown away. Whoa, I can see an afterimage.

As he flies parallel to the ground, his body splits into an upper and lower half. His upper half corkscrews into the air, growing smaller until it flies out of sight. The lower half crashes into the ground, sending up a cloud of dust before continuing to roll, but it stops dead with its feet aimed at the sky.

He may be weak to physical blows, but this is what happens when Lammis really punches something, huh? She certainly is powerful. If she can learn to control her destructive potential, she'll get even stronger.

"Whoa, did you two just end this by yourselves?"

The other members seem to have finished taking down the skeletons. They all gather around us. I go back to my usual vending machine form.

Mikenne manages to grab the King of Souls's skull, which barely remained after he flew far away, and brings it to us. Short drags over the upside-down lower half.

Over half of him is annihilated, but now we have the rest of the only slightly destroyed parts of the King of Souls in one place.

"This thing's still just barely alive, eh?"

Captain Kerioyl puts a foot on the skull and looks down at it. He must be implying that he'll crush it the instant he detects any strange movement.

"To...step on...a great one...such as I...warrants death... A thousand deaths..."

"You talk pretty big for someone about to kick the bucket. I'll just crush you, take the coin, and be on my way."

"The coin... Fu-ha-ha-ha... You all... Do you think I'm a mere...stratum lo—?"

"Get away, everyone!"

Suddenly, the captain shouts, his face changing drastically, as he kicks away the nearby Fools and jumps back.

The Band of Gluttons raise their first "Vaaaaahhhh!" in a while and flee in every direction.

I don't get it, but it's time to activate Force Field!

The moment the blue light envelops Lammis, our vision is covered in black.

[Points decreased by 500.]

*　　*　　*

Wh-what?! It's totally black all around us!

If my points went down, does that mean we're under attack?! What's going on? Did the King of Souls muster the last of his strength to self-destruct?!

"Boxxo, what's happening? A-are we okay?!"

That's what I'd like to know, Lammis. After hearing her confused voice, I regain a little clarity. Panicking will get us nowhere. I have to calmly judge the situation.

[Points decreased by 500.]

The decrease isn't stopping. Is this blackness one of his spells or something? Based on how the Force Field feels, it seems to be coming down from above.

After withstanding it for a while, the black torrent fades, and we can finally see light again. The darkness raining from above seems to have stopped. My points have stopped going down, too.

"No... E-everyone's..."

When the darkness fades, we see an enormous crater in the ground. We're in the center of that crater, and the only ground left is under our feet. The land is warped in an incomprehensible way that you'd never normally be able to imagine.

Our party... They're facedown in the dirt, scattered about the outside edge of the crater. They're not dead—at least, I hope not.

They've probably just passed out, since most aren't moving. The captain and Mishuel, though, are struggling to somehow get to their feet. Those two are alive, at least. No doubt about that.

"Oh? To think there were some who could withstand my dark magic," says a voice from above.

I look up and see a skeleton about two sizes bigger than the King of Souls floating in the air. The silver skeleton is clad in a hooded robe, but the robe's embroidery is more intricate than the King of Souls's was, and despite being worn by a skeleton, it exudes a sense of nobility.

He has four arms, and behind him I catch glimpses of something else—a tail made of bones?

"Talentless disciple. I will have returned to me the dead one's arm that clings to the light."

The floating skeleton points his palm downward, and the ground in the crater rises up. The buried King of Souls's staff rises into his hand.

"Superior magic items should belong to superior beings… Do you not think so, visitor from another world?"

That glittery silver skeleton has figured out my identity? When he looks at me with those dark eyes, I feel a chill, as though he's seeing through to my very vending machine core.

I don't know who he is, but he must be a higher-ranked being than the King of Souls we defeated.

"Wh-who are you?!"

"Hmm. My name has been lost to time, but I suppose most call me the Netherlord. I am also the one who rules over the filth you call the King of Souls."

I thought as much—he's an upgraded version. In this situation, one wrong move will be our last. Among our comrades, we don't know if the Band of Gluttons or the red-and-white twins are alive. Captain Kerioyl and Mishuel are the only ones managing to hold on to consciousness. What should I do to save them? What can I do?

If I just want to save Lammis, all I need to do is hold out with Force Field. I still have a point surplus. Quite a few points flowed into me after defeating the King of Souls, so I'm confident I can defend against anything.

But I couldn't save the others. Should I forsake them…?

"So this is the so-called coin of a stratum lord. Hmph. A worthless trinket."

With a simple finger gesture, the coin floats in front of the Netherlord. But then the coin falls, as if he's lost interest in it, brought down by gravity.

"Wh-why did you do this?!"

"Why? Is there a problem with my hunt? You assaulted the King of Souls to fulfill your own ambitions as well, did you not? I had thought surprise attacks were the specialty of you lowly hunters."

"Y-you're right, but—"

"As I recall, there is an expression in the world of man that goes: Do unto others as you would have them do unto you. Even children know it."

"B-but that's—"

"That's what? Are you saying this is any different? I would very much like to ruminate if you would tell me what about it is different. Well, human?"

This bastard is teasing Lammis. He's playing around. This is the kind of superfluity someone with absolute power shows to the weak. Normally, this would be our chance to strike back to some extent, but I can't see any possible outcome where we win this.

What I Can Do as a Vending Machine

Isn't there a way to overcome this situation using only my features?

The enemy is descending from the sky to the ground. What will work on him?

Lure him into the crater he made himself, then suffocate him with dry ice poured in beforehand... That would be pointless. Skeletons don't breathe. Besides, he could just escape into the air like before.

Nothing edible would have any effect. I can't expect anything from ice or water, either. Maybe we do need to start thinking about giving up. Escape should be the number one idea in our minds.

But how are we supposed to flee in this situation? If we can distract him, we might be able to do something, but...

"Uwoohhhh!"

With a cutting shout, a red flash appears to run from the crown of the Netherlord's head to the ground—but it's just Mishuel, who brought his greatsword down on him.

He's all right!

"That was an illusion. But you were very close, black-armored young man."

"Hah...hah... So surprise attacks won't work after all."

Mishuel's breathing is ragged, and he's barely managing to stay upright by using his greatsword as a staff.

There's no way he's all right after that attack. He must be at his absolute limit to have gotten in a strike at all.

"Well, well. Foul play against evil. Does it not sting your conscience? What is the true face of justice, I wonder? Hmph."

The Netherlord shrugs and swings his tail around. Mishuel, without any energy to dodge left, takes the hit in a defenseless state and crashes to the ground.

"Oh. I suppose you can't enlighten me."

"Quit trying to have a discussion with that talkative bastard!"

Suddenly, I hear a voice— It's Hulemy! That's right, she and Shui were farther away in the buar cart, so they're still unharmed.

After her angry shout, several plastic bottles reach us. They're flying in a straight line at the Netherlord.

Immediately, I realize what she's doing and erase just the plastic bottles, using the same trick as before to try to splash their contents all over the Netherlord.

"The highly flammable oil? Hmph."

With only a small puff of air, the Netherlord creates walls of wind at his sides. He must intend to blow the diesel away.

"Not yet!"

With Shui's words comes a fire arrow flying through the air, igniting the diesel— No, it's gasoline. It explodes before hitting the wind wall.

"Lammis, Boxxo, get out of there while you have the chance!" shouts Shui.

"Hurry!"

Urged on by their words, Lammis kicks off the ground and jumps to the crater's edge. I don't forget to turn into a cardboard vending machine to lighten the load for it.

"Captain, Mishuel, get on, quick. We've gotta scram!" cries Shui, stopping next to the two as they struggle to get into the buar cart to push them inside.

"I'll help, too," says Lammis, leaping over in a single bound, easily tossing them in.

"We're running for now!" yells Hulemy.

"But everyone else is—"

Hulemy sets off before waiting for a response, and Lammis reluctantly follows.

When I look behind me, the rest of our comrades are still lying on the ground. After blowing away the flames, the Netherlord, now floating in the air again, looks contemptuously at them, for some reason unmoving.

What's going on? Is he going to let them live, since it's not worth killing them? Whatever the reason, if they survive, that's fine. We just have to get away.

"And where might you be going? You still haven't told me."

The skeleton's condescending speech speaks directly to my brain. It's kind of like Telepathy, one of the Blessings.

Everyone seems to have heard him, but they don't turn around. They speed up.

"My, my. Didn't anyone ever teach you to look at someone when they're talking and listen until the end? Young people these days know nothing of manners."

Now he's talking like an old man from the countryside. If he was just an annoying old man complaining about courtesy, that wouldn't be a problem, but when the Netherlord with all his ridiculous strength says it, it's a different story.

I don't know how far Telepathy can reach, but if he's just going to talk to us and not attack, then I don't care how much he talks to himself.

"You're abandoning your comrades?"

Suddenly, without any warning, the Netherlord appears in our way. I guess things are never that easy.

This isn't the sort of enemy we can kill in a hit-and-run way. Hulemy knows that, and she pulls the reins to try to change course.

"If you can't have a conversation, doesn't that make you little more than animals?"

For whatever reason, the staff he's holding disappears, and he brings his empty hands out in front of him. I don't know what he's doing, but I have a bad feeling about it. I put up a full-power Force Field and watch closely, lest I miss even the slightest movement.

His silver fingers, without a scrap of skin on them, close slightly— and then Hulemy and Shui appear in his hands.

"Hulemy! Shui!"

They were just in the driver's seat— Why are they there? I look at the buar cart, but it's empty now.

The Netherlord is floating in the air, gripping their necks. They're swinging their arms and legs, trying to resist somehow, but the Netherlord doesn't react at all.

"You, the girl with the amusing Blessing and the magic item with the soul of an outsider. You two are interesting. For that, I will let you live. You still have much growing to do, so I think I can expect great things from you in the future."

"Let them go!"

Lammis, emotions flaring, jumps in. I want to stop her, but if I forced her to stop right now, she'd regret it for the rest of her life. Even though I know this is a taunt to lure us in, we have to go!

"You're aware of the overwhelming difference in our power, and yet, still you struggle. Good, good. I admire your resolve. I particularly enjoy the songs about the adventures of those called heroes. An evil-vanquishing hero's road to power is paved with the deaths of comrades. And I must play the part of the villain!"

"N-noooooooooooo!"

The worst-case scenario unfolds in my mind. I'm currently a cardboard vending machine on her back, so I'm not weighing her down. She's advanced the distance of several steps in just one jump. And yet—

"Hearts dance in turmoil. Revel in death."

The instant the Netherlord says those words, darkness wraps itself around Shui's and Hulemy's bodies, and they both give a massive jerk.

Then he lets them go, and they begin to fall to the ground upside down.

"Uwaaaahhhh!"

Lammis digs her heels in and explodes off the ground, dust erupting behind her. She crosses over thirty feet in a single leap, slides underneath them as they fall, and catches them before they collide with the ground.

"You did well to make it in time. As a reward, I will return their corpses to you. I anxiously await your growth. I will remain in this stratum for a time. You may come for revenge whenever you like."

Leaving us with that, the Netherlord raises his staff and vanishes from sight.

"Hulemy, Shui, answer me! Please, please...answer me..."

Does she understand the danger of slapping them in the face with her Might? She simply stays next to them, tears falling, clenching her fists.

The two girls look like they're just sleeping, but given how disturbed Lammis is, I don't plan on being enough of an idiot to think about it that optimistically.

"Hulemy, you promised you'd always help me out... Shui, everyone...everyone at the orphanage is waiting for you... So please...please, seriously, please!"

"That piece of shit... My comrades... You bastard!"

"Not...not again..."

The buar cart must have caught up. Mishuel and the captain cry out in grief.

Mishuel is using his sword to barely stay up on one knee, but blood is dripping from his bitten lip.

The captain, who can just barely move, gets off the cart and removes Shui's and Hulemy's armor and clothing.

What is he doing at a time like this?! I want to yell at him, but I'm misunderstanding— He starts to do a cardiac massage on Shui.

"Lammis! You learned basic hunter treatment for people whose hearts have stopped! Don't just stand there!"

"R-right!"

Lammis puts me to the side. Then, being careful not to put too much strength into it, she begins to massage Hulemy's heart.

Please be all right!

She's got a bad mouth, but she's been supporting Lammis like a big sister. She understands me, too. She's important to me.

And Shui—bright, eats a lot, giving her all to the hunting life for the sake of an orphanage.

And now their bodies lie before me.

"No good! I can't get her to breathe!"

Lammis's cry of anguish echoes through the wastelands.

Do we have to give up? Do we really have to accept their deaths without doing anything...? No, not yet! It's too early to give up!

He said, *Hearts dance in turmoil. Revel in death.* Their corpses have no external wounds—it's like they're sleeping. If I'm to trust Captain Kerioyl's judgment, their hearts have just stopped. Which means there's still hope for saving them!

I immediately select a feature I've had my eye on and acquire it.

A clear door attaches slightly off-center on my vending machine body, and orange objects appear inside it. After they materialize, a red-heart pattern and the letters AED appear next to them.

The feature I chose is the ability to dispense an AED. An AED is an automated external defibrillator, a medical device that gives an electric shock to someone in cardiac arrest to revive them.

With the onset of so many earthquake disasters recently, vending machines that you can attach simple toilets and AEDs to for emergencies are on the rise. Thanks to that, I was able to get the feature now.

In their state, I have faith that using this can revive them!

"Huh? What's this? What?"

Noticing my change, Lammis stops her work and looks at me—the tears still streaming down her face. But she doesn't understand what it is. I don't blame her. Nobody in this other world would immediately figure out what it is just by seeing it.

Few Japanese people would recognize it at a glance. And even if they knew it was an AED, they'd hesitate to actually use it.

Reviving someone from cardiac arrest is a race against time. There's no room for hesitation!

I don't have a way to explain it to Lammis, so leaving it to her is impossible. There's a manual with diagrams inside the case, but it would still take some time to figure it out.

How many points do I have left...? About 1,220,000! That's enough!

As a result of helping kill the King of Souls and my laborious saving until now, plus the Flame Skeletitan Coin reward, I was able to save up this much.

*   *   *

The skill I should learn now—Telekinesis.

This Blessing's ability is "You can control objects within a radius of three feet. However, there is a weight limit, and you can only use it on your products."

I don't know whether the AED falls into the definition of "product," but I don't have any other choice. There's no reason to waver!

I spend one million points to acquire Telekinesis, then focus on my AED and will it to move. Sure enough, the clear door opens, and the AED comes out. Now it's floating through the air.

Good, good, good, good, we're past phase one! The next step is to open the case and take out the contents. Then, to place the yellow device on the ground and put the electrode pads on their chests... Damn, I can't reach. The three-foot limitation is getting in the way now?!

"Huh? The item is floating... Are you doing this, Boxxo? You're trying to do something, aren't you? Could it be, could it be that you can bring them back to life?"

"Welcome." I respond affirmatively to her question spoken without hope.

Lammis's eyes go wide. "R-really?! Um, you want to do something with that boxy thing with the string on it, right? Um, uhhh, do you need to get closer to them?"

"Welcome."

"Okay, got it!"

She's responding in a pretty quick-witted manner, but since I'm panicking, even that almost seems like it's wasting time. Calm down. Lammis is nearly in an actual panic, so I have to think carefully and take action.

I need to deal with this calmly. I understood everything about how to use the AED when I chose it. Now I just have to execute.

"You're here!"

She lays their bodies down basically right on top of me.

I'll reach them like this. Now... Sorry, Shui, but I'm reviving Hulemy first.

The electrodes go on her upper right chest and a little below her left side. I place them in those two locations. With only that, the AED automatically takes an ECG and decides whether or not electric shocks are necessary.

"Please do not touch the body. Now running ECG."

It has voice guidance built in, so any Japanese person would be able to use it.

"Electric shock required."

"Who's that voice? ...I can't understand what they're saying."

This one doesn't get translated from a Japanese voice? It must be because it's not actually a voice. After the voice speaks, it begins to charge electricity, and when it's done, it says, again in Japanese, *"Please press the shock button."*

Now I just have to push the red button on the device. There's no time to hesitate. I have to do Shui after this, too. The longer a person is in cardiac arrest, the lower their chances of revival are... Here I go. No, wait—there's still something else I can do to increase the possibility of success.

Betting on a slim possibility, I increase my dexterity stat. I still don't know what it's for, but if it does anything at all to improve this feature's effects or capabilities, I'll spend as many points as I have to.

I increase it by ten, twenty, thirty, then forty, spending a hundred thousand points, but it's still tolerable. Okay, I'm pressing the shock button!

"Electric shock delivered. You may now touch the body."

Her body gives a twitch from the electric shock, but I can't rest easy yet. It only happened because the electricity ran through her. Here's where the problem starts.

"Hulemy... Ah, you're breathing—you're breathing again! Hulemy, Hulemyyyy!"

"Seriously?! Then Shui, too—"

Thank goodness... Thank goodness Hulemy is all right. When I see Lammis still bawling as she continues her cardiac massage, my power nearly shuts down because of the relief, but it's not over. It's too early to be relieved—I still have Shui left.

Wait, what's going on here? I can control the electrodes more

precisely than before. Is this a benefit of my increased dexterity? With this, it's not hard to put them in the appropriate spots.

Putting my experience with Hulemy to good use, after giving Shui an electric shock...they've both started to breathe again.

A-all right! I... I did it. Phewwwwww.

"Shui, don't worry me like that, you...you idiot. Thank you, Boxxo. You saved their lives. I'm truly grateful."

Despite being so grievously wounded I expect him to collapse any moment now, Captain Kerioyl apologizes profusely to me while gently stroking Shui's head.

I think I should place a little more trust in the Menagerie of Fools. That's how strongly the captain's actions echo in my heart.

After the Devastation

"Wh-what about everyone else?!"

After confirming the two are breathing again, Lammis's crying face changes, and she bursts away. That's right. These two might be in the clear for now, but the other members aren't moving at all.

I want to believe they're alive, but I can't tell for sure from here. I'll just have to wait for Lammis to bring them here... Is praying the only thing I can do?

Lammis runs to our comrades at an insane speed and appears to check their wounds to see if they're breathing. For some of them, she sighs in relief; for others, she says something to herself under her breath. At this distance, I can't accurately grasp the situation.

It pains me, but the only thing I can do now is wait for her to return.

"Somehow, nobody else has sustained life-threatening injuries... Phew."

As he looks at the members sleeping on top of bath towels I gave them, Captain Kerioyl breathes a sigh of relief.

Some of the ones who got blown away are heavily wounded, but some healing medicine and appropriate first aid seem to have borne results. Right now, Lammis is gently bringing them into the cart.

Their wounds aren't fully healed, and it's possible the impact may have ruptured internal organs, so we need to bring them back to the settlement quickly, even if a little forcefully.

Hulemy and Shui have been asleep since then, so they're riding in the buar cart with the wounded.

"Mishuel, sorry about this, but I might need you to switch seats with me."

"I'll be fine. I feel much better, thanks to the healing medicine."

That's what Captain Kerioyl and Mishuel are saying, but neither is in good shape. They're both clearly far from okay. They know full well that this isn't a situation in which to show weakness.

It would be nice if my vending machine products included ointments and painkillers, but I've never seen medicine in a vending machine, possibly due to the Pharmaceutical Affairs Law. I hear they exist overseas, but I wasn't wealthy enough in my lifetime to go on a vacation to another country just to see a medicine vending machine.

The buar cart sets off, taking care to rock as little as possible. The biggest reason we're hurrying is so we can get them medical attention. But there's something else pushing us onward—the thought that the Netherlord could come back on a whim.

We arrive at the settlement and bring our comrades to the only medical office in the Dead's Lament stratum.

They receive appropriate care, and once the expert doctor gives a seal of approval, Lammis and I slump to the floor in an excess of relief.

But the two whose hearts stopped for a while need quiet bed rest. The others also took mental damage in addition to physical damage from that dark magic, and they won't be completely recovered in a matter of days.

They'll need to be hospitalized for a week at the very least.

Despite the situation, we didn't have the time to relax and wait for our comrades to heal. After announcing to the guild that the Netherlord has appeared, the captain and Mishuel, who had relatively light wounds, were called in by the guild master on this floor, and they're in the middle of an emergency council.

Within half a day, Director Bear and directors from other floors arrived, granting even more weight to the situation.

And before the day was up, they forbade civilians to leave or enter this stratum, and hunters began to assemble one group after another in the settlement.

Lammis was called by the council several times as well, and she told them what she'd witnessed. The directors' expressions, though, implied that things were not looking good.

With Lammis and me on standby, we stood outside the Dead's Lament stratum Hunters Association building together, lazily watching the clouds roll by.

"I wonder what will happen, Boxxo. I'm relieved everyone made it out alive, but that Netherlord was too strong for us, huh?"

"Welcome."

Overwhelming magic-based devastation. I can't think of a way to fight him, much less win.

I'm no help against something with intelligence and the ability to float. It taught me how lucky I was to have beaten the stratum lords before now.

While the resentment and hatred of our comrades nearly being killed were still in my mind, defeating the Netherlord was the only thing I could think about. But as time passed, I calmed down, and now, for better or worse, I can focus on reality.

"A four-armed skeleton... What was it? I've never heard of a Netherlord. Maybe Hulemy knows about it."

A being that rules over the stratum lord, the King of Souls. I want to know what on earth he is as well.

"You want to know who the Netherlord is?"

A sullen voice comes down to us from above. I look up and see Director Bear using his paws to massage his eyebrows in exhaustion. He's wearing a pince-nez and has a bundle of documents in one arm.

"Director Bear, is the council finished?"

"For now. Well, I needed to talk to you anyway. Boxxo as well. Come inside, and I'll explain."

He just got out of the Association meeting, but he turns right back around and beckons us inside. I'm interested in what he has to say, and I have no reason to refuse, so I follow him, carried on Lammis's back.

Director Bear opens a heavy-looking door all the way in the back and pushes it open, revealing a council room with a large round table in it.

"Take a seat wherever you like, Lammis."

We move to the closest chair, and after she sets me down, she sits right next to me.

We're not the only ones here—Captain Kerioyl, Mishuel, and nine other men and women I've never seen before are already seated.

"I don't need to explain those two. The other members here are the directors or representative directors from the Hunters Association on other floors."

I see. Some are dignified enough to be called directors, but there's one child who looks younger than Lammis—a director at that age?

Wait, everyone other than our acquaintances is staring at me with curiosity. I've gotten used to this feeling already.

"Everyone, she and the magic item are also ones who encountered the Netherlord and survived. They'll be deeply connected to our upcoming plans, so I called them here as a special exception."

"Director Clearflow, is that magic item the rumored box you can buy unknown things from?"

A young woman wearing a crimson woman's suit stares at me, twirling a fountain pen between her fingers.

"Yes, Director Origin. He is also one of our talented hunters, possessed of considerable talent and ability, who has saved us numerous times."

The directors call one another by their stratum names? I personally think Director Bear fits him a lot better than Director Clearflow.

"I see. I apologize for interrupting. I have no more to say."

"Mm. Then I'll continue. The Netherlord who has appeared is, without a doubt, the Netherlord, the left-arm general of the Demon Lord's forces."

"Oooooooh."

The cacophony of surprised voices seems somehow feigned, as though everyone already knew but was being surprised again.

"Excuse me, but what's the left-arm general of the Demon Lord's forces?"

Lammis nervously raises her hand and asks the question. I was just wanting to know that, too. Nice assist.

"It's only natural some wouldn't know. Far to the north of here is a country controlled by a being who calls himself the Demon Lord. His forces consist of several generals, but they're called different things depending on their rank. The Demon Lord himself is positioned at the head and considers his subordinates his arms and legs. From the highest rank, there's the right-arm general, the left-arm general, the right-leg general, and the left-leg general. These are the four limb generals, and below them are twenty finger generals."

In other words, a Demon Lord exists in this world, served by several subordinate generals. The second-highest-ranked one, the left-arm general, is the Netherlord.

That's a pretty high position, isn't it? He's essentially rank three in the Demon Lord's army, rank one being the Demon Lord himself, and he came all the way here. Still, there's a demon lord here, huh? I guess it would be weird for this world setting not to have one, but even so. A Demon Lord...

"We don't know why the Netherlord has appeared here, but judging by the conversation held at the scene, the King of Souls, this stratum's lord, was his subordinate. I think you all know that stratum lords can never leave the dungeon."

Really? That's the first I've heard.

"It is said that the spirits of the dead gather in this stratum and become monsters. Perhaps the King of Souls was once a human or a monster who died, and his soul came here and became the King of Souls. Or he gained entrance to the dungeon using some other method. This is all just hypothetical."

You mean all that could have happened? Based on what the King of Souls and the Netherlord said, they did seem to have a boss-underling relationship, and the Netherlord was talking like he was the boss.

"In any case, we can speculate about what we don't know once everything is over. The problem is what to do about the Netherlord, since we believe he will be staying in this stratum."

"Can I ask something, Director Clearflow?"

"What is it, Director Scorching?"

An oppressive-looking man raises his hand and speaks. He has bronze-colored skin and olive-brown hair. His clothes include a Hawaiian shirt with flames on it and pants the color of desert sand. He has the macho-man look fit for a summertime beach.

"Would it even be wise to take an aggressive attitude with an officer of the Demon Lord's forces? If we defeat him, won't that cause issues later?"

"We shouldn't have to worry about that. He was the one who came to attack in the first place. If the Demon Lord's forces want to take an aggressive stance against us, then all we can do is receive him in kind. For the Demon Lord's forces to directly invade this place, even in small numbers, they would have to destroy Bastion City or the empire first. I believe there's no doubt that the Netherlord is moving independently right now."

I don't have the geography of this world down yet, but north of this land where the labyrinth lies is an empire—a place called Bastion City— that meets the Demon Lord's forces, and unless they do something about it, it's impossible for them to come and attack us.

"Then why would the Netherlord be acting alone?"

"That I do not know, Director Origin. But there are places in this dungeon yet to be understood. When strata are breached, the— No, let's not waste time on speculation."

If the government gets involved, things will probably get annoying, but it looks like we can ignore that just fine. Well, sending him away with negotiations might actually be better for the people here.

"Anyway, what do we do about it?"

"Our only option is to kill him. He laid a hand on a member of the Hunters Association in the dungeon we supervise. We must rally our forces and defeat him."

Director Bear has the look of a calm gentleman at first glance, but the light in his eyes belies the fury of the wild. He's not about to take the defeat of the Menagerie of Fools and the Band of Gluttons, who he's on close terms with, lying down.

"Heh, it's not often I see you get this into it. Defeating monsters is part of a hunter's job. We won't have business after a humiliation like this. I'll send the skilled hunters assigned to my place into the fight."

"The Origin stratum will give several groups as well."

The conversation wraps up with the other strata volunteering their competent hunters, and the council adjourns. It looks like this will be a battle on a large scale.

Maybe a group of extremely skilled hunters would be able to beat the monster, too.

"Lammis, Boxxo, Captain Kerioyl, and Mishuel. You've done well. You've all heard this council's decision. Now, I'd like to ask you personally. Do you intend to participate in the hunt for the Netherlord?"

"'Course I do. He won't get away with putting my Fools through that."

"Please allow me to participate as well. This battle made me painfully aware of my own inexperience. Allow me to repay this humiliation!"

Captain Kerioyl's and Mishuel's wills aren't the least bit broken. In fact, they're gushing with fighting spirit.

I look to Lammis next, who hasn't said a word since the council began. She brings her downcast face up with force. There is no fear or hesitation in her expression, just strong, swelling determination.

"I'll be part of this, too, of course! He hurt everyone and put Hulemy through that… I won't be satisfied unless I get in a good punch! Right, Boxxo?"

"Welcome."

Yeah, that's right, Lammis. We'll show him our power.

"I see you're all zealous about this. I will prepare the best people we have assigned to the Clearflow Lake Hunters Association. We will work with them, and we will kill the Netherlord."

Director Bear sticks out a fist, and the others follow suit. It's only at times like these I find myself wishing I had arms.

Epilogue

I go outside with Lammis, and we sit down in the town square near the inn. I've been let off her back and placed next to her.

The sky in the Dead's Lament stratum is dark again today—the weather looking dismal, as usual.

"I'm happy everyone's safe, but this is still hard."

"Welcome."

Maybe we should celebrate everybody making it through such a strong enemy with their lives, but in the midst of all our comrades getting hurt and falling, I'm reminded that the only thing we could do was run away.

I was confident I was helping everyone by being a little convenient and increasing my stats, but that confidence has faded after what happened.

When all's said and done, I'm a vending machine. I can protect with Force Field, but that's it. I have neither the hands to hold a weapon nor the feet to run into battle with them.

I leave all the striking to Lammis, too, while I just use Force Field. I had mistakenly thought that was enough to be of assistance to them.

"Too bad." My voice unconsciously comes out.

"Boxxo, you're not thinking it's your fault everyone got hurt or anything, are you?"

Lammis's words rattle me, and my vending machine lights flicker off for just a moment. I don't know how much my lights blinking conveys my emotional ups and downs, but she can't read my mind.

Yet, she still guessed what I was thinking and asked me about it. How is she able to nail down what an inorganic machine is thinking?

"Welcome."

"But it wasn't! That's not true!"

Lammis claps her hands around my body and pushes her forehead right up to me. Her teary eyes are lifted upward a little, and her mouth is tightly shut in apparent frustration.

Is she angry... No, is she sad for me?

"It's 'cause o' you I'm safe, Boxxo," she says in her accent. "Hulemy and Shui, too. You saved 'em! So don't go thinkin' those sad thoughts..."

She's crying for me—for a vending machine. I must be the worst man alive to make such a cute girl cry.

Lammis is the best partner I could ask for. As her partner for life, I can do plenty of other things that are better than being depressed.

"Oh. I wanted to give some encouragement, too, but I guess I don't need to."

I hear a voice behind me, so I look over. Director Bear has carried Hulemy here princess-style. She just got revived from cardiac arrest— she should need absolute quiet bed rest right now. Is it all right for her to be up?

"Hulemy, how are you feeling?!"

"I feel fine, but I can't quite muster the energy for much. I talked the director into carrying me. I had to give my thanks... Thank you, Boxxo."

Still in the director's arms, she gives a smile, but it's weaker than usual. Her physical state is probably far from perfect.

"Welcome."

"I can't help out in battle, but I don't think I'm useless. I could never compete in strength with Lammis, and Mishuel and Captain Kerioyl are better at fighting than I'll ever be. Oh, and the director is strong, too, right? Plus, we have Vice Captain Filmina for magic power. But when it comes to my skill as a magic-item engineer, I think I have everyone else beat!"

"That's right. You're handy and smart." Lammis nods in vehement agreement.

I feel the same way. I've never once thought you were useless, Hulemy.

"It's the same for you, Boxxo. You may not be able to move by yourself or fight, but you can make food and drinks, and you even have Force Field. If you start whining now that you're not strong enough, you're gonna get punched. No, I'll have Lammis punch you as hard as she can!"

"Too bad." I'm sorry. Please spare me that. I won't get depressed anymore.

After hearing my response, Lammis and Hulemy exchange glances and break out into grins.

"We're the ones who should be down in the dumps here, not Boxxo."

"My own inexperience... I'm truly pathetic."

Captain Kerioyl and Mishuel break into the conversation.

Their faces still don't look great, but they participated in the council, so they've probably recovered enough so that they have no obstacles to daily life.

They walk over to us with firm gaits. Behind them are the rest of the Menagerie of Fools, as well as the Band of Gluttons.

Their wounds are all closed, but their exhausted stamina won't return immediately, so their steps are unsteady. Still, even wobbling, they walk under their own power.

Vice Captain Filmina, who didn't take part in the battle, is waiting in the back, worried about her comrades.

They were all supposed to be having total rest. Why are they out here?

"These guys wanted to thank you, too, Boxxo," says Captain Kerioyl, prompting everyone to give me a hard, serious stare, then all smile at once.

"You've saved the captain and our members, Mr. Boxxo. As vice captain, you have my gratitude."

"Seriously, thanks. I already decided that when I die, it'll be resting my head on a beautiful woman's lap!"

"Right! Thanks to you, we don't have to call off that dream!"

Vice Captain Filmina bows deeply, and the red-and-white twins give me thumbs-ups with their right hands and wink.

"As the leader, let me say thank you, Boxxo."

"Yeah, you saved us."

"Now we can eat as much fried meat as we can stomach."

"All you think about is food, Pell. You have to say thank you, okay?"

The Band of Gluttons all stand shoulder to shoulder, holding one another up. Personally, just seeing you do something so adorable is the best thanks I could hope for.

"You saved me when I was about to die, right? Thanks, Boxxo."

Shui, propped up on the red-and-white twins' shoulders, leaves them and jumps at me, practically falling into me. She hugs me and then gives my body a kiss.

"It's not much, but here's my thanks!"

As I stand there baffled, she blushes a little and gives a mischievous grin.

"Huh?! What are you doing, Shui?!"

"L-look, you…"

Lammis comes over and peels Shui off.

They seem to argue with each other, but Hulemy slides smoothly in front of me and stares at the place Shui's lips touched.

"Guess I have to thank you, too," she says, gently pressing her lips to me like Shui did.

"Ahhhhh, Hulemy, not you too!"

Gripped under the arms, Hulemy is easily carried away.

She sets her down right next to Shui. Lammis's cheek is puffed out. She must be complaining to them.

To think I'd be kissed by two people. Maybe this world is less like Japan and more like overseas countries, where kisses are a form of light greeting. Even so, as a man, it makes me happy.

"I swear… And you look pretty happy, too, Boxxo!"

Lammis stands in front of me, pouting. She must have finished her lecturing.

"Don't get it twisted," she continues, slipping into her accent again. "That was just affection and gratitude. It's not like they're sweet on ya or anything!"

Yes, I'm fully aware.

"I can't believe they went and did a fool thing like that…"

If her accent came out, that means she's rattled.

"That's not just something you can up and do. Uh, but if it's as thanks, then there ain't no harm in me doin' it, too, right? Y-yeah, I've gotta show proper thanks, like Ma always told me."

H-hold on, Lammis?

Her face flushes bright red as she wraps me in a tight embrace, straightening up and bringing her face closer.

Ohhhh, h-her face, her lips are just barely—

"N-nope, I can't do it after all! I'm comin' down with a case of the vapors!"

She dug in at the last moment. Her face is so red I can almost see steam rising from her ears.

Whew, that surprised me. To be honest, I'm also a little disappointed, but this outcome is more like Lammis, right?

So I tell myself, with a sigh of relief, but…

"Come on. Your self-consciousness isn't doing you any good, as usual."

"You just gotta get it over with."

Hulemy and Shui go behind Lammis, and smiles appear on their lips before they give Lammis a push on the back.

"Huh? Mmm—"

Losing her balance, Lammis falls forward, and her soft pink lips press firmly against me.

Urgh. If I had a sense of touch, I'd be happier. But I'm happy enough with this. She's making me blush.

"Eh, I, wh-what was that, Hulemy? Shui?!"

Lammis panics, turns around, and closes in on them.

If I had a physical body, I'd probably have a blissful smile on my face. Those depressing feelings are nowhere to be found now.

If I were a normal human with arms and legs, we'd probably be able to have more fun together.

But this body is how I'm helping everyone. I've been reborn in another world.

In that case, I just have to do what I can as a vending machine.

"Hah. All that yelling made me thirsty. Boxxo, can I have something good to drink?"

"Me too."

"I want some food, too!"

The two girls Lammis was angry with come back to me again and begin earnestly picking out products behind the glass.

"W-we want some, too!"

"Then us too!"

Even the Band of Gluttons and the red-and-white twins came over.

They form a line without giving me time to respond. Shrewdly, Director Bear, the captain, and the vice captain join at the end of the line, too.

All right, time to switch gears and do what I'm supposed to as a vending machine reborn in another world!

"Welcome."

Afterword

This is the third volume, so there's no one new I have to introduce myself to, right?

But betting on that one-in-ten-thousand chance—it's a pleasure to make your acquaintance. My name is Hirukuma. For those of you reading this afterword in Volume 3, or perhaps Volume 4, it's good to see you again. How did you like Volume 3?

There's a lot more Shui in this book than before. We get to see an unexpected side of a girl whose traits include tomboyishness and being a heavy eater.

She might seem like she has too much in common with Lammis, who is also tomboyish and full of energy. But in this volume, we learn that in addition to Shui's particular manner of speaking and her appetite, she turns out to have been a big-sister character all along.

Mishuel also appears as a new character, one who is good-looking, strong, and seems to have a tranquil personality. This is my own work, so even characters who seem perfect tend to have a quirk to them.

Personally, I quite like his personality. I think that if he were around as a real-life friend, there would be some problems, but it would be fun.

And then *he* shows up at the end. Stories always need to have someone like this, of course.

Other than that, in terms of the story, I'll touch on the eating contest.

We have all these big-eater characters in the Band of Gluttons as well as Shui, so I wanted to have them take the spotlight. If they were to participate in an eating contest in Japan, the organizers would probably lose a lot of money. If it were me, I wouldn't let them in.

That said, I'd like to express my appreciation for all the people involved with this book.

I continued the unreasonable requests of having a vending machine as the main character and, since Volume 2, Tasmanian devil beast people, but there were no conspicuous, colorful characters this time, were there? Thank you as always for your wonderful illustrations, Ituwa Kato.

To M, my editor, I know you're busy with advertising and editing, but please take care of yourself. And to everyone else in the editing department, I hope I can thank you with my books' appeal.

Once again, my mother has been advertising to my relatives and friends every chance she can get. My older brother and his family, too.

I'd like to thank all my friends, too. If you'll allow me to say one thing to them: Quit calling me sensei on purpose.

And to all my readers who purchased this book, thank you very much!

Hirukuma